HAVE THIS ONE ON ME

Set against the background of the City of Prague and the frontiers of the Iron Curtain, this is the third episode in the chequered career of *Mark Girland*—the layabout secret agent whose weaknesses are money—and women . . .

HAVE THIS ONE ON ME is another exciting, compulsive novel from the maestro of thriller writers.

Also by James Hadley Chase

and published by Corgi Books

Have This One On Me

James Hadley Chase

CORGI BOOKS

HAVE THIS ONE ON ME
A CORGI BOOK 0 552 11309 3

First published in Great Britain by
Robert Hale Ltd.

PRINTING HISTORY
Robert Hale edition published 1967
Robert Hale edition reprinted 1977
Corgi edition published 1980
Corgi edition reissued 1986

Corgi Books are published by Transworld Publishers Ltd.,
61-63 Uxbridge Road, Ealing, London W5 5SA,
in Australia by Transworld Publishers (Aust.) Pty. Ltd.,
26 Harley Crescent, Condell Park, NSW 2200, and in New
Zealand by Transworld Publishers (N.Z.) Ltd., Cnr. Moselle
and Waipareira Avenues, Henderson, Auckland.

Made and printed in Great Britain by
Hunt Barnard Printing Ltd., Aylesbury, Bucks.

Have This One On Me

The Caravelle from Prague touched down on schedule at Orly airport, Paris. Among the passengers to leave the aircraft was a short, thickset man in his middle forties. His round, fleshy face was nondescript, his steel grey eyes restless. He wore a drab brown and black check sports jacket, grey flannel slacks and a brown straw hat that rested on the back of his head. He carried a black, well-worn briefcase which he had nursed on his knees during the hundred minute flight.

This man's name was Jonathan Cain. He held an American passport and had a two-room office on Rue Paul Cezanne off Rue du Faubourg St. Honoré. His business was exporting fine glass to various important galleries in New York and Washington. Every other week, he flew to Prague where his orders for glass were received with respect and attention. The Czechs needed foreign currency and Jonathan Cain represented a steady and important source of foreign currency revenue.

Leaving the bus that had taken him to the Arrival Centre, Cain walked briskly into the building, passed through the police control and the Douane with a brief nod of recognition from the coloured official, and then out into the hot sunshine where he hailed a waiting taxi, telling the driver to take him to Rue Royale.

As the taxi pulled away, Cain looked back through the rear window, his eyes alert and searching. No other taxi had moved from the rank, but he was not satisfied. He continued to look behind him as his taxi began to race

7

along the Auto-route that would eventually lead to the traffic-choked streets of central Paris.

Cain had every reason to be cautious, for apart from being a glass exporter, he was also one of the most reliable couriers working for the Central Intelligence Agency in Paris. His job was to keep contact with various agents behind the Iron Curtain, to pass on information, to take messages back to Paris and to keep tabs on the work of the agents, making sure they were earning their money and making doubly sure none of them had become blown.

He was returning from Prague with disturbing news. He seldom contacted John Dorey, the Divisional Head of C.I.A. branch in Paris. It would be fatal to him if he was seen with Dorey, but the situation was such that he now had to see Dorey. He had to be certain that he wasn't being followed.

But seeing the mass of traffic now behind him, Cain shrugged and settled back in his seat. The time to lose anyone following him would be when he reached Rue Royale.

Thirty minutes later, the taxi swirled around the Arc de Triomphe, stormed down Avenue des Champs Elysées, forced its way round Place de la Concorde and finally reached Rue Royale. Cain got out, paid the driver, then walked towards Place de la Madeleine. At the corner of Rue Royale and Bd de la Madeleine was a luxury glassware shop. Cain entered. He walked down the long aisle, flanked on either side by tiers of cut-glass, nodded to the blonde saleswoman who gave him an automatic smile of recognition, and entered a small office where Jacques Foy was talking on the telephone.

Foy, young, effeminate and blond with a sunlamp complexion, glanced up, nodded and went on talking in a shrill, petulant tone.

Shutting the door, Cain took off his sports jacket and his hat, opened a closet, hung the jacket and hat on a peg, took out a blue blazer and shrugged himself into it. From a shelf, he took a green and cream straw hat which he put on. Then waggling three fingers in Foy's direction, he opened a door at the rear of the office and carrying his black brief-case, walked quickly down a narrow alley that led into Rue Duphot. Here he picked up a taxi and told the driver to take him to Chez Joseph, Rue Cambon.

Joseph Fevret, the owner of the restaurant, greeted him as he entered the small bar. The two men shook hands, then Fevret, portly, balding with a close clipped moustache and beard, led Cain up the narrow stairs and into a small, private dining-room. The table set for two stood by the window. White lace curtains obscured the diners from inquisitive passers-by in the street below.

'I hope you had a good trip, Monsieur Cain,' Fevret said. 'Is there anything special you would care to have for lunch?'

Cain dropped his hat on a chair, wiped his face with his handkerchief and shook his head.

'I'll leave it to you, Joseph. Something special.'

'I suggest Moules farcies en cocotte. A half a bottle of my special Chablis. Then Tournedos Massena with a half a bottle of Ausone 1945,' Joseph Fevret said, knowing that Cain always wanted the best and expected the best. He had given some thought to the suggested meal during the morning.

'Sounds fine,' Cain said. He glanced impatiently at his wristwatch. The time was twelve forty-five. 'When my friend arrives, bring him right up.'

'Of course, Monsieur Cain.' Fevret bowed and left the room.

Cain sat down away from the table and lit a cigarette. His heavy face was thoughtful. A few moments later, a waiter came in with a double Vodka martini which he placed on the table. He bowed to Cain as he left the room.

Cain ate the olive, flicked the cocktail stick into the fireplace and then sipped his drink. He again glanced at his watch. He was shooting his cuff back into place when the door opened and John Dorey came in.

Dorey, with thirty nine years of service at the Paris American Embassy behind him, now held the exalted rank of Divisional Director of the C.I.A. Aged sixty-six, he was a small, bird-like man, wearing rimless spectacles. He looked more like a successful banker than the shrewd, ruthless head of an extremely efficient organisation that was in continual battle with the Russian espionage network.

'Hello, Jon,' Dorey said as he closed the door. 'You're looking pretty good.'

'Think so?' Cain shook hands. 'I wish I felt it.'

There came a discreet tap on the door and the waiter came in with a Cinzano Bitter, soda and ice which he offered Dorey. Cain knew this was Dorey's drink, and Dorey, taking the glass, nodded, pleased.

When the waiter had gone, Dorey drew up a chair and sat down.

'Has something happened?' he asked with deceptive mildness.

'An understatement,' Cain said. 'Worthington's blown.'

Dorey stroked his beaky nose. He sipped his drink, then shook his glass slightly, making the ice cubes clink.

'Your man in Prague?'

Cain took out a packet of Marigny cigarettes. He was used to Dorey by now. Dorey always liked to have the set-up explained to him from an outside angle as if he wasn't aware of all the facts.

'Alec Worthington,' Cain said patiently. 'English. Married to a Czech. Lived in Prague for ten years. Teaches English to various political leaders. We bought him three years ago. He has a bug about acquiring capital—who hasn't? We pay his earnings into Credit Suisse Banque, Bern. He has saved around sixty thousand dollars. Up to now his information has been useful and he has earned his keep. Somewhere along the line, he must have made a false move. Probably he was over-confident. Now, he is suspect. He could bluff it out as I am sure there is no proof against him, but he's lost his nerve. The money he has saved haunts him. He wants to get out and spend it. Can't say I blame him, but that's not much use to us. He's a mess now. We will have to replace him. He plans to bolt.'

Dorey finished his drink as the door opened and the waiter wheeled in a trolley. The two men moved to the table. Dorey's eyes were blank behind the glittering lenses of his glasses, but when a plate was set before him, he became alert, regarding the Moules farcies with approval.

'Joseph's is probably still the best unknown restaurant in Paris,' he said. 'These look very good.'

'Yeah.' Cain began to eat. He was sure Dorey wouldn't attempt to solve his problem until after the meal.

Later, when the Tournedos Massena arrived with the Château Ausone in a cut glass decanter, Dorey said, 'You are spoiling me.'

'Okay, if that's the way you feel,' Cain said and poured the wine. 'I'm spoiling myself too.'

The two men finished their meal. There was little conversation. Dorey asked after Cain's business. Knowing he wasn't interested, Cain didn't elaborate on the subject. He said business was pretty good and left it at that.

It was only after the coffee had been served and the waiter had finally left them that Dorey said, 'I never did think much of Worthington. Well, all right . . . I'll find a replacement.'

'I don't envy your replacement,' Cain said seriously. 'The red light's up. It's tough out there now. They have a Russian security man tightening up their system . . . a man called Malik.'

'Malik?' Dorey looked up, his eyes narrowing. 'Oh . . . yes. He's probably one of the best and the most dangerous of them. So Malik is out there, is he?'

'He's the reason why Worthington has panicked and wants to get out.'

'Do you think Worthington will get out?'

Cain shrugged.

'I don't fancy his chances. Anyway, I am sure he will try. The last time I saw him he was falling to pieces badly.'

'When do you think he will try?'

'I don't know. Right now he is screwing up his courage. It's my bet, once he makes a move to get out, they will grab him.'

'Haven't we got a woman out there?'

'Mala Reid.'

'Yes, I thought so. She's good, isn't she?'

'She has been useful.'

'Under pressure, Worthington will talk.'

'Yes, he'll talk all right.'

'That could be awkward for you and Mala?'

Dorey sipped his coffee. His mind was busy, but his expressionless face didn't reveal the intensity of his thoughts. Cain watched him.

'I don't want to lose Mala, and I certainly don't want you to lose your contacts in Prague,' Dorey said eventually. 'Perhaps we could do something about Worthington.'

There was a long pause, then Cain said quietly, 'The only thing we could do of any use would be to kill him. Once Malik gets hold of him, there's nothing we can do. Mala and I will automatically be blown.'

'That's something we must avoid.' Dorey finished his coffee. 'It's not as if we owe him anything. He's been useful, but he has been well paid. It would have to be done quickly, wouldn't it?'

'Not later than tomorrow night.' Cain stubbed out his cigarette. 'Even tomorrow night might be too late.'

'I think I have his address. It's the same?'

'Yes.'

'He lives there with his wife?'

'Yes.'

Dorey thought, then put down his coffee cup. He looked cold and remote.

'I will arrange it.' He stared at Cain. 'In the meantime you had better keep clear of Prague. Have you any reason to think Malik suspects you?'

'No one suspects me,' Cain said with quiet confidence. 'I'm the white-headed boy who brings in the dollars.'

'Don't be too sure. Malik is dangerous.'

'So long as you shut Worthington's mouth, I'll be all right.'

Dorey nodded.

'His mouth will be shut. Now about a replacement . . .' He thought for a long moment. 'There's Jack Latimer. He speaks the language. He's been working for International Calculators now for the past two years. I could get him transferred to Prague with no trouble. What do you think?'

Cain poured more coffee into his cup.

'If Malik wasn't there, I'd say yes. Latimer is a good man, but I have an idea Malik will smell him out before he can get set. The red light is up. They know you will be replacing Worthington. Any newcomer will come under a microscope.'

'Never mind about that. Could you work with Latimer?'

'Of course.'

'All right. I'll arrange it.' Dorey got to his feet. 'Thank you for a beautiful lunch, Jon. You do nothing now until I give you the green light. In a couple of weeks—with any luck—you will be able to return to Prague and contact Latimer. I am sure he will be much more useful to us both than Worthington.'

Cain shook hands. He knew Dorey well enough not to ask further questions. If Dorey said he would fix something, he did it.

He watched Dorey leave, then finished his coffee and rang for the bill.

* * *

Alec Worthington closed the lid of his suitcase and snapped down the catches. He looked at his wristwatch, then walked over to the window. He peered through the net curtains down into the narrow street. The squat man in a short black raincoat and slouch hat was still leaning against the wall, his hands hidden in his coat pockets. He had been there now for the past four hours.

Worthington stepped back and dabbed at his sweating temples with his handkerchief. Again he looked at his watch. The time was five minutes to ten. In five minutes Suk would be arriving for his English lesson. When Suk arrived, the watcher would go. Suk was the second in charge of the Czech Secret Police. So long as he was with Worthington, there was no need for the watcher to remain. When Suk had finished his lesson, the watcher would return. All this Worthington knew. The terrifying routine had been going on now for the past four days. Now, this day, Worthington had decided he must go. Time was running out. He felt the pressure. Even now, he might have left it too late. He felt instinctively that they might arrest him at any moment.

But he wasn't ready. If there had been more time, he could have followed his original plan, but he knew they were almost ready to take him. He had to run to cover.

He pushed the suitcase under the bed, then he walked into the small living-room. He was tall, slightly built; a man in his late forties. His grey-black hair was thinning. He was unmistakably English with his hooked nose and his closely clipped military moustache.

Emilie, his wife, had gone out shopping. She wouldn't be back for at least two hours. Every shop had its queues, and shopping for food was a long, serious business in Prague. He felt no pang about leaving her. When he had first met her, some fifteen years ago, he had thought her the most exciting woman in the world. During the passing years, she had grown fat and had become dull minded. Love had left them and he couldn't remember when they had had intercourse together. The thought of that made him wince. All she could think of was food and where to find it. As far as he knew she had no idea that he worked for the C.I.A. and that he had accumulated a reasonable fortune in Switzerland. Nor, as far as he knew, did she know that there was another woman . . . nor did the other woman know that Worthington had fallen in love with her.

He crossed to his desk: a poor piece of furniture, rickety, scratched, with numerous cigarette burns on its unpolished surface. He opened a drawer and took from it a cosh he had made from a piece of sacking. It contained sand. and pieces of lead he had picked off the sloping roof while Emilie slept. He balanced the weapon in his hand, his heart beating uncomfortably. He wasn't a man of violence. He hated violence, but now his life was threatened. He had no alternative but to resort to violence.

He slid the cosh into his hip pocket, then he sat down at his desk. He was surprised that he was so calm: it was a calm of fatality. The lesson today, he remembered, was a reading from Galsworthy's *The Forsyte Saga*.

14

Although he hated and feared Suk, Worthington had to admit the Czech was showing promising progress. His accent was now acceptable. It was surprising that a man of his brutal reputation should find such obvious pleasure from the very English Forsytes.

Worthington opened the well-worn book and found the place where Suk had left off the previous day. He was thankful to see his hands were steady. As he placed the book on the desk, he heard footsteps on the bare wooden stairs that led to his fourth floor apartment. Wiping his hands on his handkerchief, he went to the window and looked again into the narrow street.

The watcher had gone.

The front door bell rang. Putting away his handkerchief, he went to the door and opened it.

Suk nodded to him and walked past him into the living-room . . . a fat, bulky man with thin lips, stony, suspicious little eyes.

'It is a fine morning,' Worthington said automatically. 'The sun makes it pleasant to walk. Please be seated, Mr. Suk.'

'It is a fine morning and it is pleasant to walk,' Suk said, putting his black, greasy hat under the chair. He stared at Worthington as Worthington moved around his desk and picked up the Galsworthy novel. 'I hope your wife is well.'

'She is very well, thank you,' Worthington said, knowing this was an exercise in English and that Suk had no interest in his wife. 'I hope your wife is well too.' He handed the book to Suk.

'Yes, she is well,' Suk said. He crossed one fat leg over the other. 'Thank you,' he added as an after thought.

'Well, let us commence,' Worthington said, trying to steady his voice. 'Shall we continue to read? You did very well yesterday. I have marked where you should begin.'

Suk again stared at him, settled his bulk into the chair and holding the book away from him, began to read. Worthington, his hands behind him moved slowly around the room. He wondered if Suk could hear how violently his heart was pounding. The muscles in his legs were twitching. He wanted badly to sit down, but this had to be done quickly. It could be his làst and only chance of freedom.

'One moment,' he said, pausing. His teacher's instinct for perfection over-rode the urgent need for action. 'Do you undèrstand what he means by that sentence? Will you read it again?'

In his heavy voice, Suk read, ' "Dry up! Don't I tell you he's taken the knock?" ' He stared at the printed pages, then he scowled, shaking his bald head. 'No, I don't know what it means.'

'Dry up means stop talking,' Worthington explained, his fingers touching the cosh in his hip pocket. 'Taking a knock means he has had a misfortune. Do you understand now?'

'Yes,' Suk said.

'Then please go on.' Worthington began to move around the room. He was now behind Suk. His sweating fingers drew out the cosh. He stared at the enormous bald head. What thoughts, he wondered, were going on under that bony structure? Was Suk really planning to arrest him and hand him over to Malik?

Suk was reading a descriptive passage of Soames For-syte in court. He suddenly stopped as if he had a premoni-tion that something was about to happen. He began to turn his head as Worthington, his breath whistling between his teeth, struck him.

The sand-filled canvas bag smashed down on Suk's head. The canvas split, showering sand and bits of lead over the carpet. Suk remained motionless, his great head low on his chest, sand trickling down the top of his bald head, around his flat ears and on to his scurfy collar. Holding the limp, empty strip of canvas, Worthington watched him in horror. Then the squat body seemed to become boneless. Suk slid off the chair and his fat body thudded to the carpet, an inert mass of flesh and shabby clothes.

Worthington dropped the strip of canvas and ran un-steadily into the bedroom. He snatched out the suitcase from under the bed, grabbed up his black mackintosh that was now a uniform in Prague and ran back into the sitting-

16

room. Suk still lay where he had fallen. Worthington wondered in terror if he had killed him, but there wasn't a moment to lose. He left the apartment and began to walk quickly down the four flights of stairs.

As he was descending to the first floor landing, he heard someone coming up. He paused, hesitating. There was nowhere to hide. He knew if the person coming up was one of his neighbours, he or she would be immediately curious about the suitcase he was carrying. He was still hesitating, in an agony of indecision, when Emilie, his wife, came into sight.

Emilie, now forty-four, was a short, enormously fat woman with blonde dyed hair that looked like a discarded bird's nest, whose blue eyes were buried in a layer of fat and whose shabby summer dress struggled desperately in its attempt to confine her bulging figure.

They stared at each other.

Emilie's eyes went to the suitcase and then she looked at Worthington who was smiling fixedly, wondering if he would have to kill her.

'So you are leaving?' she said. She always spoke in Czech to him. 'Don't look so frightened. Do you think I care?'

He drew in a long slow breath, realising in his desperation to get away, he could have killed her. 'Yes, I'm leaving,' he said, his voice shaking. 'Good-bye, Emilie. I hope it works out for you. Don't go up yet . . . do some more shopping.'

She moved her heavy shopping basket from one hand to the other.

'So you are finally going to join your whore?' she said. 'Good riddance! I've been waiting for this moment. I am glad to see you go.'

Worthington flinched.

'I'm sorry . . . you'll be all right. Your father . . .'

'Don't tell me what to do! Go to your whore,' and turning she began to plod up the stairs to the next landing.

'Emilie! Don't go up!' Worthington's voice shot up in panic. 'Do more shopping. I—I had to hit him . . . he's up there.'

17

She paused and regarded him.

'You fool!' Her voice was full of contempt. 'Do you imagine you will get far?'

Worthington realised he was wasting time. He looked at her, feeling this was the last time he would see her. He looked from her to the red cabbage showing through the network of her shopping bag. She was always partial to red cabbage.

'Good-bye, Emilie.'

The last he ever saw of her as he glanced back was a picture that fitted her so well, clutching on to the basket of food, her eyes screwed up, her face cold. As he reached the door to the street, he heard her plodding down the stairs after him. She would go back to the market and then return with more food. He didn't blame her. Life in Prague now centred around food.

He walked quickly down the narrow street, his eyes searching every doorway. There was no one to see him go. They had been so sure that so long as Suk was with him, reading Galsworthy, he wouldn't attempt to escape.

At the end of the street, Worthington paused at a tram stop, falling in behind a long queue of people who waited with the passivity of cattle for the tram to arrive.

As he waited, he wondered how long it would be before Suk recovered and began a relentless and deadly hunt for him. It depended, Worthington thought, on the thickness of Suk's skull. He grimaced as he thought of the violence of his blow.

The tram clanged to a standstill and there was a surge forward. There was no hope of a seat and Worthington found himself wedged against an elderly man who looked at him and then away. Worthington's obvious English appearance made the man suspicious, but this Worthington was used to. People in the streets, hotels and restaurants always looked curiously at him. They knew by his shabby clothes that he couldn't be a tourist. Ever since he had lived in Prague, he had been the subject of suspicion.

When the tram reached the Town Hall square, Worthington got off. He walked briskly past the famous clock, constructed in the 15th century by Hanus of Rouze. Already tourists were assembling to watch the statuettes of the Apostles and of Christ appear when the hour struck. He looked up at the figure of Death the Reaper which would toll the passing of time, and slightly quickened his step, knowing that his own time was threatened.

Working his way through the crowds that thronged the sidewalk, he turned down a narrow street, flanked on either side by restyled Baroque buildings until he came to a courtyard. Here, he paused and looked back over his shoulder. An old woman, limping, her gnarled knuckles white over the handle of her stick, was coming towards him. He and she were alone in the street. He walked into the courtyard, skirting a moss covered fountain that had long ceased to function and then, with another furtive glance over his shoulder, he stepped into a dark doorway and began to mount steep wooden stairs.

On the top floor, a little breathless, he walked down a dimly lit passage and stopped outside a shabby door. Again he paused to listen, then satisfied no one was coming up the stairs, he pressed the bell push.

He heard a movement behind the door, the sound of a key turning, then the door swung open.

He always experienced the same surge of excitement when he saw Mala Reid. He had been in love with her from the time they had first met, but he had never given any indication of his feelings. He knew by her attitude, by the way she received him that she regarded him merely as a man who delivered messages as she would regard the postman and now as she looked inquiringly at him, her dark eyebrows lifting, he again realised how impersonally she regarded him.

'Why, hello . . . what are you doing here?'

Worthington entered the big studio, set down his suitcase, took off his hat and shed his raincoat. While he did so, he regarded the girl who had shut the door and was leaning against it, her expression worried.

Mala Reid was twenty-eight years of age. She had been born in Prague of American and Czech parents. Her father, the Czech, had been executed during the revolution. Her mother had died some three years ago of generalised cancer. Mala now made a reasonable living as a singer at the Alhambra night club. Her voice wasn't anything very much, but with the aid of a microphone, she managed to satisfy not-too-critical tourists. She did have a small talent for imparting feeling and sensuality into the songs she sang, and the American tourists liked her. This was a qualification that the Government encouraged. Because of her, extra dollars were earned. She had been singing now every night at the club for the past two years.

She was above average height. Her hair was tinted to the colour of sable. She was attractive without being beautiful. She had high cheek bones, large violet coloured eyes, a full lipped mouth and a long, thin nose that turned up slightly to give her a cheerful, gamine look. Her body was her biggest asset: full breasted with a narrow waist, solid hips and long sensual legs. Her body kept the eyes of the tourists occupied while they scarcely listened to her voice.

Two years ago, one of Dorey's agents had persuaded her to work for the C.I.A. Although she was of normal intelligence, the agent felt she didn't realise into what danger and into what situations, his sales talk was leading her. She was strongly against regimentation, against Communism, and it seemed to her the obvious thing to agree to help. Up to now, she hadn't done a great deal to help. She had passed messages on to other agents, she had worked with Worthington, not knowing how involved he was and how close to danger he was living. Three times, during the past two years, without understanding what was happening, she had given the C.I.A. vitally important information. They had marked these achievements to her favour although she had been merely a postman. Back in Paris, Dorey's opinion of her capabilities were exaggerated. Had she known that she was now regarded as the best woman agent in Czechoslovakia, she would have been utterly dismayed.

Because she had lived all her life in Prague, was a good dollar earner and knew how to behave herself, she was regarded by the Security Police as a good citizen. She was completely suspicion-free and therefore a perfect tool for Dorey.

Worthington's sudden appearance startled her. The time was eleven-ten in the morning. She had just got up and was finishing a cup of coffee. She was wearing a faded housecoat, her bare feet in pink mules. She looked from Worthington to the battered suitcase he was carrying.

'Are you going away?'

Worthington took out his handkerchief and dabbed his temples.

'Yes. Sit down, Mala. I want to talk to you.'

'Is something wrong?'

Worthington thought of Suk's crumpled body lying on the floor in his sitting-room with *The Forsyte Saga* by his side. He looked at Mala, feeling a pang of pain and frustration. Even at forty-seven, and after eight years of celibacy, Worthington could still think regretfully of the pleasure a girl like this, with her body, could have given him. Comparing her to Emilie, remembering his wife's gross fat and her meanness sickened him.

'I have to stay here for a few days,' Worthington said as Mala, looking bewildered, sat down. 'I'm sorry . . . I have to. There are things I have to do. There are things you must do.' He leaned forward, his face twitching. 'I have to stay here.'

'Stay here?' Mala gaped at him. 'But there's no room! You—you can't possibly stay here!'

'I have to. I promise you I won't be a nuisance. It is only for a few days, then I will be leaving Prague. Without your help, I can't leave.'

'But there is only one bed.' Mala waved to the small divan standing in an alcove. 'You can't stay here!'

How simple it would be, Worthington thought bitterly, if she offered to share her bed with me. But why should she? She doesn't love me. Who am I to her?

'I can sleep on the floor . . . there's nothing to worry about. You can trust me . . . I just have to stay here.'

Mala regarded him, her eyes opening wide. Seeing how white he was, seeing the lurking fear in his eyes, she said, 'Are they looking for you?'

Worthington nodded.

'Yes,' he said.

21

Captain Tim O'Halloran leaned back in the chair. Tall, broad shouldered with light blue eyes, a hard mouth and a red fleshy face, he was in charge of all the C.I.A. agents in Europe and was Dorey's right hand man.

Dorey, sitting behind his desk, fiddling with a paper knife, had told him of his meeting with Cain. O'Halloran had listened, his hard face expressionless, knowing that Dorey would come up with some kind of solution. He had tremendous faith in Dorey.

'So there we have it,' Dorey said, putting down the paper knife. 'If Malik catches Worthington, both Cain and Mala Reid will be blown. Worthington must be liquidated. Who can do it?'

'Mike O'Brien,' O'Halloran said without hesitation. 'He can fly out tonight on a diplomatic passport . . . no trouble at all. By late tonight or by tomorrow morning, he will fix it.'

Dorey frowned, thought, then shrugged.

'All right, Tim . . . go ahead . . . fix it,' he said and waved to the telephone.

He drew a bulky file towards him as O'Halloran began to dial a number. He was still reading the file when O'Halloran put down the receiver.

'You can consider it done,' O'Halloran said quietly.

Dorey nodded and continued to read. O'Halloran sat back and waited. While Dorey examined the file, his thin face tight and pale, O'Halloran thought back on the years he had worked under this man. He was perhaps a little kinky to O'Halloran's thinking, but there was no doubt that he was brilliant, shrewd and utterly ruthless when the cards went down. O'Halloran decided in the brief minutes that it took Dorey to sign his name on the clipped in page of the file that he would rather work for Dorey than anyone else in the C.I.A.

Dorey pushed the file away and then looked up, his eyes studying O'Halloran through his bifocals.

'We now have to replace Worthington,' he said. 'I think Jack Latimer would do, but Cain isn't optimistic. They will be watching for a replacement. Cain thinks Latimer could get blown before he even started.'

'Latimer is our man,' O'Halloran said. 'Suppose I talk to Cain?'

'I've talked to him. Cain always makes sense.' Dorey put his fingertips together. 'Malik is there. Do you remember Malik?'

'Who doesn't?' O'Halloran said, straightening in his chair.

'Yes . . . Malik is the Soviet's best man. Well, at least, we know he is there. So . . .' Dorey paused to study his fingernails, his eyebrows coming down in a frown. 'We have to fool Malik and get Latimer into Prague.'

Knowing Dorey had already solved the problem, O'Halloran said nothing. He waited.

'We must create a smoke screen,' Dorey went on. 'We will put an obvious agent into Prague and while Malik is working him over, Latimer slips in.'

O'Halloran rubbed his fleshy jaw.

'Sounds fine, but the obvious agent as you call him will have it rough.'

Dorey smiled bleakly.

'Yes, certainly but he will be expendable.' He paused and regarded O'Halloran, then went on, 'Did you know Girland is back? He arrived from Hong Kong this morning.'

'Girland?' O'Halloran sat forward. 'Back here?'

'Yes. I keep tabs on Girland. He owes me a lot of money. It is time he paid me back.' Dorey picked up his paper knife and examined it. 'I am going to use Girland as my smoke screen. When Malik hears Girland is in Prague, he will jump to the conclusion that Girland is our replacement. While he is working Girland over, Latimer will slip in. How do you like the idea?'

O'Halloran stared down at his freckled hands while he thought. He had considerable respect for Girland who, at one time, had been Dorey's best agent.

'What makes you think Girland will go to Prague?' he asked finally. 'Girland no longer works for us. He is no fool. I can't see him going behind the Curtain.'

23

'Girland has two weaknesses: women and money,' Dorey said. 'He will go. I guarantee it.'

'If he does, you will lose him. Do you want to lose him?' Dorey's thin lips tightened.

'Girland thinks only of himself. He has worked for us only because he has made a profit out of us. He has managed to swindle me out of quite a large sum of money. It is time we made use of him as he has made use of us. So we lose him . . . it will be no great loss.'

O'Halloran shrugged.

'If you're smart enough to get him to Prague, then it is no skin off my nose what happens to him. I don't have to remind you he's a smart cookie. Just why should he go to Prague?'

'If the bait is tempting enough, the fish always bites,' Dorey said. 'I have a beautiful tempting bait for Girland. He'll go to Prague.'

❊ ❊ ❊

Worthington came out of the tiny bathroom, dabbing his face with a towel. He had shaved off his moustache and his lean face now looked longer and weaker.

'It makes quite a difference,' he said. 'I have worn a moustache for twenty-five years. I feel rather lost without it.' He took from his breast pocket a pair of horn rimmed spectacles and slipped them on. 'Wearing these and without my moustache, I don't think they can possibly recognise me, do you?'

Mala stared hopelessly at him. The moustacheless upper lip and the glasses had changed his appearance. The way he had taken over her apartment, the way he had assumed that she would help him had left her stunned.

'I thought I would bleach my hair,' Worthington went on, peering at himself in the mirror over the fireplace. 'I have a bottle of peroxide in my bag. I'm not sure how to use it.' He turned and looked inquiringly at her. 'Could you help me?'

Mala drew in a long shuddering breath.

'No . . . I won't help you!' she said, trying to control

her voice. Terror was mounting inside her. She knew if they caught Worthington, he would betray her. That long weak face warned her there was no steel in him. Once they began to interrogate him, he would tell them everything. Then they would come here and take her away. The thought of being in the hands of the Security Police, what they would do to her, made her sick with fear. 'Please go. I mean it. Please . . . please go!'

Worthington looked reproachfully at her.

'You don't mean that,' he said. 'Suppose I make you a cup of tea? Tea is so much better than alcohol.' He looked vaguely around. 'Where do you keep your tea things?'

Mala gripped the arms of her chair.

'Will you please go! I don't want you here! I won't help you! Please go!'

'Now, don't be silly,' Worthington said. He removed his spectacles and carefully put them in his breast pocket. 'If they catch me, they will catch you. Let's have some tea.'

He went into the kitchenette and Mala heard him put on the kettle. She looked desperately around the room as if for a means of escape. She wanted to run out of the apartment, but where could she run to? She now bitterly regretted listening to Dorey's agent, with his smooth talk of patriotism, her duty and the money she would make. Up to this moment, she hadn't realised to what she had committed herself. Now, all the ghastly stories she had heard of what happened to spies when they were caught, crowded into her mind. Suppose she called the police? Would they be lenient with her for betraying Worthington? She knew they wouldn't be. She imagined their hot, cruel hands on her body. She thought of the outrageous things they would do to make her talk. Even if she told them everything she knew—and it wasn't much—they would still go on and on, sure she was holding something back.

Worthington came out of the kitchenette, carrying a pot of tea.

'When I have bleached my hair,' he said, setting the teapot down on the table, 'I want you to take photographs of me. I have a camera with me. I need a photo for my passport.' He went back to the kitchenette and returned with cups and saucers. 'Then I will ask you to go to an address I will give you.' He began setting out the cups and saucers. 'The man there will put the photo on my passport. He is an expert. Once all that is done, then I can go. They don't know I still have a British passport. With my changed appearance, I should be able to get out as a tourist.' He lifted the lid of the teapot and stared at the tea. 'I do miss China tea,' he said and sighed. He replaced the lid, 'Do you take milk?'

Mala stared at him, shrinking back in her chair. She had to bite her knuckles to stop herself screaming.

*　*　*

Mike O'Brien arrived in Prague by car at nine o'clock p.m. He had flown by air taxi to Nurnberg, picked up a car and had driven fast to Prague.

O'Brien, young, sandy haired, flat faced with freckles and with ice-grey eyes was O'Halloran's hatchet man. During the three years he had worked for O'Halloran, he had been called upon to execute four agents who were on the point of defecting. These executions were now routine to him. He had no compunction about taking human life. Even his first killing had left him unmoved. To him, it was merely a job to be done: a ring on the door bell, the silenced gun, the squeeze of the trigger. He had decided from the start that a head shot was safest. With a .45 slug, a man's brain would be immediately shattered.

He had studied a street map of the City. He had no trouble in finding Worthington's apartment. He parked his car, slid out, slammed the door shut and walked briskly into the apartment block. As he ascended the stairs, he touched the gun hidden in his pocket. With any luck, he told himself, he would be back in Nurnberg by midnight. He would spend the night there, then fly back to Paris.

He reached Worthington's floor and before he rang the bell, he snicked back the safety catch on his gun. He made sure that it would slide out of his pocket, then he dug his thumb into the bell push.

There was a brief pause, then he heard footsteps and the door swung open.

A giant of a man confronted him. This man had silver-coloured hair, cut close, a square shaped face, high cheek bones and flat green eyes.

O'Brien felt a shock run through him as he recognised Malik. He hadn't met him before, but he had seen his unmistakable photograph in the dossier the C.I.A. had of him.

O'Brien looked beyond Malik. Three men, two of them holding Sten guns, all wearing dark, shabby suits and black hats, were staring at him, motionless and menacing.

Malik said, 'Yes?' His voice was polite, the flat green eyes expressionless.

O'Brien's mind moved swiftly. Had they caught Worthington? It looked as if they had. Why else should they be in the apartment?

'Is Mr. Worthington here?' he asked. 'I understand he gives English lessons.'

'Come in,' Malik said and stood aside.

O'Brien hesitated, but the threat of the Sten guns warned him of his danger. He moved into the shabby living-room. The three men, behind Malik, continued to stare at him, continued to remain motionless.

'Mr. Worthington is not here,' Malik said closing the door. 'May I see your passport?'

With a slight shrug, O'Brien produced his passport and handed it to Malik.

'How is Mr. Dorey?' Malik asked as he tossed the passport to the man without a gun.

O'Brien grinned.

"He's not dead . . . that I do know. How is Mr. Kovski?' This was the name of Malik's chief.

'He's not dead either,' Malik said. There was a pause, then he went on, 'You are a little late. Worthington left here about ten o'clock this morning. Please tell Mr. Dorey that I will take care of Worthington. Assure him that Worthington will not escape.' He gave a stiff little bow. 'I am sorry you have had a wasted journey. If you will please accompany this man, he will return your passport at the airport.'

The short, bulky man who had put O'Brien's passport in his pocket, moved to the door. O'Brien accepted the inevitable. He followed him.

'One moment, Mr. O'Brien,' Malik said. 'Please don't return. You wouldn't be welcomed. Do you understand?'

'Sure,' O'Brien said. 'So long.' He walked past the bulky man and headed for the stairs. As he did so, he heard the muffled sound of a woman sobbing somewhere in the apartment. This would be Worthington's wife, he thought, mentally shrugging. He wouldn't want to be in her shoes.

Malik!

He grimaced.

chapter two

'Look, kitten,' Girland said, 'in five minutes I have to
go out. Would you please finish your drink and then put
on your skates?'

The girl sitting opposite him swished the dying ice cubes
around in her glass. Girland had picked her up at the Left
Bank Drug Store. She was scarcely eighteen and sensation-
ally beautiful. Dark, sensually built, wearing scarlet stretch
pants and a red and white shirt, she had caught Girland's
roving eye, but now he had her back in his apartment on
Rue des Suisses, he realised too late that she was too
young, too eager and too generally too.

'Are you telling me to get the hell out of here?' she
asked, looking inquiringly at him, her head on one side, a
pose she copied from a movie star who impressed her.

'Sorry, but that's it,' Girland said with his charming
smile. 'I have to go out.'

'Don't we do anything? I'm good. What's the rush?'

Girland sighed. Why in the world, he wondered, do I get
myself into these kind of situations? The trouble with me is
I never know when to say no. She looked marvellous.
Damn it! She *is* marvellous! Why is it when most women
open their mouths, they become the biggest bores? If she
had only kept her mouth shut, she could have been a sen-
sational lay.

'I invited you for a drink. You have had your drink.
Now I have to go out.' He got to his feet. 'On with your
skates, kitten!'

She nibbled at her drink, her full lips pouting. She
looked up at his tall, broad shouldered figure, his lean

hard face and the scattered white hairs in his jet black hair. What a bull of a beautiful man! she thought.

'You're not serious, are you?' she asked. 'I had the idea you and me were going into action. Back home, they call me Swivel Hips. I'll give you an unforgettable experience, boyfriend. At this moment, there's nothing between us but the zipper on my pants.'

Girland studied her. She made him feel middle-aged. This eager, brash sexual approach was like ice water thrown in his face.

'Some other time perhaps,' he said. 'Fold your tent, kitten, and steal away.'

The telephone bell rang.

'This I love,' the girl said. 'Every time I get close to a real man, the goddamn telephone starts up.'

'That's life,' Girland said, picking up the receiver. He waved to his front door. 'That's the way out: down the stairs and you will find the Metro on your left. So long, kitten.'

A voice over the line, speaking with a strong New Yorker accent said, 'Girland?'

'I suppose so,' Girland said and dropped back in his chair.

'This is Harry Moss,' the voice told him. Behind the voice Girland could hear distant swing music. 'You wouldn't know me. Fred gave me your number.'

The girl walked over to Girland and emptied the dregs of her drink over his head. Two dying ice cubes bounced on his shoulder and slid to the floor. Carefully, she balanced the upturned glass on the top of his head and then walked to the door, swinging her small, firm hips. Sighing, Girland took the glass off his head and put it on the side table. He waved to the girl who gave him a V sign.

'Fred . . . who?' he said into the receiver.

'I've a little job you could handle if you felt like it,' the voice went on. 'It means money.'

Thinking of his empty wallet, Girland became attentive. 'How much?'

'Bullion up to your navel,' the voice told him. 'Want to talk about it?'

Girland looked across the big studio at the girl who had opened the front door. She smiled at him, then zipped down her stretched pants and peeled them off. She began to pull the shirt over her head.

'Sure, but I can't talk now,' Girland said hurriedly. It was just possible his concierge might be climbing the stairs. He could imagine how she would react if she saw what was going on on his landing. The girl had shed her shirt, and now in only a pair of black briefs, she was striking a pose.

'I'll be at La Croix d'Or until ten. You know it?' the voice went on.

'Who doesn't?' Girland said. 'I'll be there,' and he hung up.

The girl struck another pose.

'Like me?' she said and smiled invitingly.

Girland liked her very much, but she was still too young and too brash.

'Gorgeous,' he said. 'Thanks for the show. There's a launderette at the end of the street. Wash your mind, kitten, it needs washing.' He hurriedly slammed the door and turned the key. He stood for some moments listening to her screams of rage and the names she hurled at him through the panels of the door. He was appalled at the extent of her vocabulary. Finally, she ran out of words and breath and he heard sounds of her dressing. He wondered what his neighbours were thinking. Finally, he heard her stamp down the stairs.

He lit a cigarette and sat down.

Who was Harry Moss? he wondered. Fred? The only Fred he knew was the barman at the Bressane bar where Girland went frequently. He telephoned the bar and asked for Fred.

'This is Girland.' There was the usual exchanges about their health and how life was, then Girland said, 'Know anything about a guy who calls himself Harry Moss?'

'That fella.' Fred sounded disapproving. 'Sure, he blew in a couple of hours ago. Young—around twenty-three—could be a fag, but I wouldn't swear to it. I wouldn't trust my wife with him: come to that, I wouldn't trust my mother with him either. He wanted a job done . . . I wouldn't know what it is. I got the hint it was smuggling. I didn't know how you were fixed so I gave him your name. Did I do wrong?'

'No. Thanks, Fred. Every door is a door of opportunity. If something jells, I'll see you get a slice off the top,' and Girland replaced the receiver.

He sat for some minutes thinking. He needed money. When didn't he? he thought wryly. In fact, face up to it, Girland, he said to himself, you need money damned badly. That was a mistake staying in Hong Kong for so long.* He thought of Tan-Toy and sighed. What a girl! The Chinese girls certainly had technique. He had remained with her until the money he had gypped Dorey out of had been spent. He had been thankful he hadn't cashed in his return air ticket otherwise he would have become a D.A.S., and Dorey would have loved that. Well, let's see what Harry Moss has to offer, he thought and got to his feet. You never know. Life is still full of surprises. Bullion up to your navel, Moss had said. Girland grinned. What a way to talk!

La Croix d'Or was a sleazy night club off Rue du Bac. Girland had been there a few times. It was the haunt of ageing homosexuals, and generally, it was crowded with blond handsome boys looking for a client. There was also a Negro trumpeter who had the talent of a minor Armstrong. Very few women frequented the club, and those who did were unquestionably dykes.

As Girland walked down the dimly lit stairs that led into the cellar club, he could hear the golden notes of the Negro's trumpet. He nodded to the doorman who gave him a blank stare, then entered the smoke laden room. The smell of body sweat, the noise of shrill voices and the golden notes of the trumpet made an impact on him. He paused, looking around the crowded room, then edging past the blond boys who were shrilling and looking like gaudy parroquets, he reached the bar.

*See *You Have Yourself A Deal* (French title *La Blonde de Pekin*).

The balding barman, fat and simpering, came quickly towards him.

'Yes, dear?' he said, laying his puffy white hands on the bar. 'What can I make you happy with?'

'Hello, Alice,' Girland said and shook hands. He knew the barman liked to be known by his professional name. 'Harry Moss around?'

'Yes, dear. He's waiting for you.' The barman rolled his eyes. 'Such a lovely boy! He's upstairs . . . room 4.'

'Is he alone?' Girland asked.

'Of course, dear: he's waiting for you.'

Girland grinned.

'Be your age, Alice. You're getting your lines crossed.' He shouldered his way across the room, opened the door and climbed stairs. He paused outside room 4, knocked and walked into a tiny cubicle where a youth was sitting at a table, a bottle of Scotch, two glasses and an ice bucket before him.

Girland closed the door.

'Moss?'

The youth looked around. His thick blond hair rested on the collar of his cowboy shirt. His small green eyes, his hooked nose, his thin mouth added up to a portrait of depraved viciousness.

'Come on in,' he said and waved to a chair. 'Yeah, I'm Harry Moss.' He had a strong New Yorker accent. 'Glad to have you here.'

Girland sat down. He flicked out a Pall Mall cigarette and set fire to it.

'You called . . . I'm here . . . so let's make it snappy,' he said.

The green eyes roved over Girland's face.

'I have a job I can't do myself. It's strictly dishonest, but there's no blow back. The take is thirty thousand dollars. Half to you, half to me. You interested?'

'I could be,' Girland said. 'You'll have to convince me there's no blow back.'

'I've asked around,' Moss said, staring at his glass. 'You sound like the guy to help me, and brother! I need help.' He sipped his drink, then squinted at Girland over the rim

33

of his glass. 'I'm telling you because I have to. I can't stop you flapping with your mouth, but they said you didn't talk.'

'They?' Girland asked, amused.

'I told you . . . I've asked around.' Moss again stared at his glass. 'I'll put you in the photo. I got drafted into the goddamn army. Before I got over the shock, I was in West Berlin. Can you imagine? My divisional officer was such a dummy he could scarcely write his name. One of the jobs he had to do was to collect the payroll for the Officers. I drove the payroll truck while he sat on his fat fanny and looked important. A pal of mine, Ferdy Newman, went along as a guard. Well, to make this short, we decided to hi-jack the payroll. What the hell? It was asking to be hi-jacked. So one day, a month ago, we did the job. We had to tap my officer, but we didn't hurt him much. His skull was solid bone. So we found ourselves with fifty thousand dollars and a lot of heat.' He sipped his drink and looked thoughtfuly at Girland. 'Boy! Was the heat fierce! Well, keeping it short, we got to East Berlin. Ferdy had the bright idea of moving to Prague, and from there eventually to Cairo where he had friends.' Again he paused, and this time he looked sharply at Girland. 'You interested or am I boring you?'

'Keep going,' Girland said. 'I'm never bored when any-one's talking about money.'

Moss's thin lips curved into a smile.

'That goes for me too. Well, we finally made it to Prague. They were right on our tails. The Czech Security Police came after us. We thought the heat was fierce be-fore, but Boy! did it get white hot!' Moss frowned and shook his head. 'A girl in West Berlin had given us the name of a contact. Did he turn out to be a snake! He hid us in an apartment and took twenty thousand dollars off us. The deal was he should supply us with food, keep us hidden and get us out of Prague when the heat cooled off. He certainly put us in this apartment and he certainly took the money, but that was it. We never saw him again. We stayed in that joint for three days, starving. You ever been without food for three days?'

'Why should you care?' Girland said. 'Keep talking.'

'Yeah . . . well, by the fourth morning, we were ready to eat each other,' Moss said. 'So we tossed up and Ferdy lost. He went out to buy food. He hadn't been gone three minutes when I heard police whistles. Did I lay an egg! I imagined he would bring them right to me. I beat it up on the roof. I was in such an uproar, I forgot to take the money with me.' He paused to pick his nose, then went on, 'From the roof, I saw Ferdy running like hell. There were two cops after him. They were running like elephants with ingrowing toenails. Ferdy was going like a streak. Then one of the cops lifted his automatic and let Ferdy have it. I saw bits of his shirt fly off his back and blood.' He grimaced. 'Well, that was the end of Ferdy.' He took another drink. 'I panic easily. I went down the fire escape, touching one step in six. Right at that moment, I had forgotten the money. I just blew.' He paused. 'You want to give me a cigarette? Don't if you don't want to.'

Girland tossed his pack of Pall Mall on the table. His face was thoughtful. This story could be true. Then again, it could be a lie, but why tell him if it was a lie?

'I won't bore you with details,' Moss went on after he had lit a cigarette. 'There was a girl . . .' His thin lips curved into a sneering little grin. 'What would creeps like me do without a girl? Anyway, she got me out of Prague and here I am. I've been here two weeks biting my nails. All I can think about is that money waiting for me in Prague.'

Girland sipped his drink.

'Is that all?' he asked.

'That's the story . . . that's the problem. The money's still there. I want someone like you to go to Prague, pick it up and bring it back here. We split the take. Fifteen thousand to you . . . fifteen thousand to me.'

'How do you know it's still there?' Girland asked.

'It's there. That's one thing I'm certain about. We hid it where no one would think of looking for it. It's all in one hundred dollar bills . . . three hundred of them. It doesn't take up too much space.'

'What gives you the idea I can get it if you can't?'

'They're watching for me . . . they aren't watching for you. Maybe you don't know it but Prague is the softest touch of the Iron Curtain. The Czechs are in a financial mess. They must have foreign currency so they love tourists. You go in as a tourist, stay two or three days, pick up the money and then come out. It's that simple. They don't even check the bags of tourists. I tell you . . . they love them.'

Girland stubbed out his cigarette while he thought, then he asked, 'Suppose I do find the money, what makes you think you'll ever see any of it?'

Moss grinned.

'It's a gamble. I haven't a hope of getting the money myself. So how am I worse off? It wouldn't be that safe for you to gyp me. Sooner or later, I would catch up with you, and then you would be in trouble.'

Girland leaned back in his chair, his smile widened.

'Or you would be, Harry,' he said. 'I'm tricky when little boys like you try to make trouble.'

Moss grinned amiably.

'Oh sure. I've asked around. You're tough, but I would have a try. Anyway, it's a gamble. What do you say?'

'I'll think about it. Where's the money hidden?'

'I'll tell you that when we meet at the airport and when you show me your air ticket.'

'Who's paying for the trip? I'll need at least two thousand francs.'

'Yeah, I've thought of that. I can dig up two thousand francs.'

'Well, I might do it,' Girland said. 'Suppose you call me tomorrow morning around ten o'clock?' He got to his feet. 'I'm not sold on the Iron Curtain. I don't like it.'

'That makes two of us,' Moss said. 'You talk around. Anyone will tell you, for a tourist, it is dead easy.'

'I'll do just that. So long for now,' and Girland left the room.

Moss finished his drink. Then he went down to the Club room. Pushing his way to a telephone booth, he shut himself in. He dialled a number. After a delay a curt voice said, 'Yes?'

'This is A for Apple,' Moss said. 'Your party is deciding by tomorrow morning. It's my bet, he will go.'

'I thought he would,' Dorey said and hung up.

* * *

Girland was also telephoning. Opposite La Croix d'Or was a café. He had gone there immediately, and was talking to Bill Lampson of the *New York Herald Tribune* whose encyclopedic knowledge had often been useful to Girland.

'Hi, Bill, I'm back,' Girland said. 'How's life?'

'Is that Girland?' Lampson said. 'Well, for Pete's sake! I thought you were lost for good . . . and I repeat . . . for good.'

'Don't take it so hard. Paris is big enough for both of us . . . so what's biting you?'

'Nothing yet. How was Hong Kong?'

'Fabulous!'

'How were the girls?'

'Fabulous!'

'Is it true what they say about Chinese girls?'

'If you mean what I think you mean the answer is no, but they are definitely to be recommended.' Girland thought of Tan-Toy. 'I'll say that again.'

'Are you calling me to make me envious or is there something else?' Lampson asked.

'A little information, Bill. Can you confirm that there was an Army payroll robbery in West Berlin around three or four weeks ago?'

There was a pause, then Lampson said, 'Do you know something?'

'I'm asking you, Bill. Don't play hard to get.'

'Yeah, you're right. Two conscripted men got away with fifty thousand bucks.'

'Know who they are?'

'Harry Moss and Ferdy Newman. The cops are still looking for them. There's a rumour they got behind the Iron Curtain. What's all this about? You know something? Listen, Girland, this could be big news.'

37

Girland gently replaced the receiver. So it looked as if Moss was telling the truth. Thirty thousand dollars! He walked thoughtfully to his car. What had he to lose? Moss said he would pay his expenses. Even if the money wasn't there, a trip to Prague would be interesting. He decided he would go.

He drove back to his apartment. There would be a visa to take care of, he reminded himself, but that shouldn't take long. With any luck, he could get off in three or four days.

He spent ten minutes circling before he found space to park his Fiat 500, then he started the long climb to his apartment. Finally, he reached the seventh floor. Here, he paused.

The girl in the red stretched pants was sitting on the floor, her back against his front door. She was hugging her knees, and she looked up at him with a cheerful, jeering smile.

'Hello, boy friend . . . remember me? You've had a burglar.'

Girland contained his irritation with an effort.

'I told you to go,' he said. 'I'm busy right now. One of these days, when you have grown up, we could have fun, but not right now . . . run away.'

'Are your ears clogged with wax?' the girl asked. 'You have had a burglar.'

'Okay, so I've had a burglar. Thanks. Up on your skates, kitten and disperse like a wisp of smoke.'

'A big, heavily built man with a red, fat face,' the girl went on, continuing to hug her knees. 'He's lost the lobe of his right ear. He was a pro. You should have seen the way he coped with your door lock. I was sitting on the stairs up there.' She pointed a finger. 'He didn't see me. It was like a movie.'

Girland became alert. A big, heavily built man with a missing right ear lobe had to be Oscar Bruckman, one of O'Halloran's toughs. There couldn't be two men with missing right ear lobes interested enough to break into his apartment.

'I see at last you are showing interest,' the girl said and

38

levered herself to her feet. 'My name's Rima. Let's go in and start afresh.'

Ignoring her, Girland unlocked his front door and walked into his apartment. He looked around, then asked, 'How long was he in here?'

'Twenty minutes . . . I timed him.' The girl joined him and stared around the room. 'I wouldn't have thought there was anything worth stealing in this dump.'

'Nor would I.' Girland began to prowl around the room while the girl went over to the bed and sat on it.

After a careful check, Girland decided nothing was missing. Bruckman's visit puzzled him. Maybe, he wondered, Dorey had sent Bruckman in the hope of recovering some of the money Girland had lifted off him, but this seemed unlikely. Dorey couldn't be that stupid as to imagine Girland would leave money in his apartment. Puzzled, irritated, Girland shrugged. It must be the answer, he told himself, Dorey's thinking was always mean. He now became aware that Rima was in his bed, her clothes strewn on the floor. He looked at her exasperated and she smiled pertly at him.

'Be big minded,' she said. 'You can't win all the time.'

Women! Girland thought. She was right, of course, men never could win all the time . . . not even most of the time, but just for the hell of it, he walked out of the apartment, slamming the door behind him. He ran down the stairs and into the street.

When you are that young, that eager, that stupid, then a little frustration was good for the soul, he thought.

He spent a dreary night in a fifth rate hotel. Halfway through the night, as he tossed and turned, trying to sleep, he remembered her as she posed half-naked before him.

I need my head examined, he thought, and angrily thumped the floppy pillow. Around five o'clock, he was still sleepless. He suddenly decided he was allowing his conscience to rule his life.

He hurriedly threw on his clothes and went down to his car. Then minutes later, he was climbing the seven flights to his apartment. No wonder, he thought, as he moved from stair to stair, I have no weight problem. He opened

39

the door of his apartment and moved into the big room now dimly lit by the coming dawn.

The bed was empty; the apartment was empty.

Girland grimaced, then shrugged.

He went to the bed, stripped off the sheets and bundled them in a heap on the floor, then he undressed, took a shower and lying on the bare bed, he went to sleep.

* * *

Oscar Bruckman stood before Dorey's desk, his thick fingers holding his hat behind his back.

O'Halloran, Bruckman's immediate boss, stood looking out of the window, chewing a dead cigar.

Dorey, seated at his desk, fiddled with a paper knife.

There was an uneasy tension in the room.

Dorey said, 'I don't know why it is but when I plan an operation—somewhere along the line—there is a mistake.' His voice was low and angry. 'I have had a report from O'Brien. He has failed. Worthington is still alive.'

O'Halloran turned from the window.

'We can't blame O'Brien. Cain's information came too late.'

'That's the usual excuse. Now Malik is on the scene and O'Brien has been kicked out. He can't go back. If Malik catches up with Worthington, and I suppose he is sure to eventually, then I lose two valuable agents.'

O'Halloran had nothing to say to this. He and Bruckman exchanged glances and waited.

'Well, at least Girland seems to be going to Prague,' Dorey went on. 'This is something I handled myself.' His angry eyes, slightly magnified by his bifocals, moved to Bruckman. 'What have you to report?'

Bruckman was pretty pleased with himself. He had done his job well.

'I went to Girland's apartment,' he said. 'I planted the envelope you gave me in his suitcase. Unless he takes the case to pieces, he won't find it, but they will once they have picked him up.'

'You're sure no one saw you break into his apartment?' Dorey asked sharply.

Bruckman suppressed a superior smile, knowing Dorey wouldn't stand smiles from him.

'I am sure, sir.'

Dorey brooded, then relaxed.

'Maybe I'd better explain this operation,' he said, leaning back in his chair. 'We want to get Latimer into Prague so we use Girland as a smoke screen. Malik's there and he knows all about Girland. He will assume Girland is our replacement. My problem was how to get Girland to go to Prague.' Dorey picked up his paper knife and examined it, then went on, 'A month ago, two conscripted men stole an Army payroll in West Berlin. Their names are Harry Moss and Ferdy Newman. They got to Prague. Newman was killed by the Czech police and Moss is now in jail. I have a young nephew here who is attending Dramatic School. I satisfied myself he could impersonate Harry Moss. He contacted Girland and spun him a yarn I had prepared. Girland apparently has fallen for it. He is going to Prague to collect what he imagines is the stolen payroll. It is necessary that he should find the money in Prague. This is part of the operation.' He opened a drawer in his desk and took out a package, wrapped in brown paper and sealed with Sellotape. 'This contains thirty thousand dollars.' He looked at Bruckman. 'You are to go to Mala Reid's apartment and plant this package somewhere where she won't find it. Girland will then be told where to find it. As soon as Girland finds the money you will call the Security Police anonymously and tell them that Girland has this money to pay for information he hopes to get from Worthington's contacts. They will, of course, immediately go to his hotel, find the money and the envelope you have planted on him. The papers in the envelope will tell them that Girland is an agent. The police will turn him over to Malik who will assume Girland has replaced Worthington. While this is happening, Latimer will fly in. That is the operation.' He passed a sheet of paper to Bruckman. 'These are your instructions. The operation has to be carefully timed. Now get off. When I know Girland is leaving

41

for Prague, I will alert you. Do nothing until you get my green light.'

'Yes, sir,' Bruckman said and picking up the packet and his instructions, he left the room.

Dorey replaced the paper knife on his desk, then he looked at O'Halloran.

'I wish Worthington was dead, Tim. He could complicate this.'

'Without being asked, I think the whole operation is dicey,' O'Halloran said bluntly. 'I've always thought you underestimate Girland. You could run into trouble with him. We don't even know for certain he will go to Prague.'

'That is one thing I am certain about,' Dorey said. 'He'll go.'

O'Halloran shrugged. It was his way of showing he wasn't convinced.

'Okay. Let us assume he does go. He could get away with your money. He's a very bright boy.'

'What makes you think he's so bright?' Dorey said impatiently. 'He's a small time crook and he isn't so bright. I am prepared to lose the money . . . the Czechs will get it. Girland most certainly won't. After all, it is Government money. The trouble with you, Tim, is you have an inferiority complex about Girland. I tell you . . . he isn't all that bright.'

O'Halloran thought of the times Girland had swindled Dorey out of considerable sums of money, but he realised this wasn't the time to remind Dorey.

'Well, we'll see what we'll see,' he said.

Pleased with his planning, Dorey frowned at him, then pulled a file towards him. This was his well known gesture of dismissal.

* * *

Worthington wound off the film, then opening the back of the camera, he took out the film cartridge.

'You mustn't look so worried,' he said. 'I will be gone in two days. Surely, we can get along together for so short a time?'

Mala, by now, had become resigned to the fact that she was landed with him. She had got over the first initial shock, and she was prepared to help him if it meant that she would be rid of him quickly. She had taken twenty photographs of him. Looking through the reflex lens of the camera at his weak, scared face, she began to feel sorry for him.

'I don't know how we will manage,' she said helplessly, 'but I suppose we will.'

He smiled at her. Regarding him, she decided he had been a lot more impressive with his moustache.

'Of course we will . . . two days . . . I promise . . . no more.' He handed her the film cartridge and his British passport. 'Would you take these to Karel Vlast? He has an apartment on Celetna ulice. He knows how urgent it is. He is old, but he is clever.' Worthington stroked his upper lip, experiencing a little start of surprise that there were no longer bristles to comfort him. 'You know where it is? You take a tram.'

'Yes.' Mala hesitated, then she said, 'Would you go into the bathroom, please? I have to dress.'

'Of course.'

Worthington entered the bathroom and closed the door. He lowered the lid of the toilet and sat on it.

Listening to her move around the room, he thought back to the time he had first met her. He had been alerted by Cain that there was a reliable woman agent in Prague who worked at the Alhambra night club. Cain said it would be safer for Worthington to pass his messages and information to her since Cain often went to the club and she would then pass the information to Cain. In this way, he and Cain need no longer meet.

Worthington remembered his first visit to Mala's apartment. He had with him what appeared to be a harmless shopping list, but that concealed, in invisible ink, information he wanted Cain to have. The moment he saw her, he had fallen in love with her. The comparison between her and Emilie was fantastic: one gross, stupid and disagreeable: the other, lovely, slim and gay. But he had never let Mala know his feelings. He kept reminding himself that he

43

was so much older than she was and besides he was married.

But during the two years they had worked together, he had become more and more infatuated by her. It hurt him that she was so indifferent to him, meeting him only as a means to make extra money.

Since he had been in her apartment, he was finding their close association a great strain. He wanted her. His body ached for her, but he knew it would be fatal even to give her a hint of his love for her. Not once, during the time they had been together so intimately had she shown anything but a wish to see him gone.

With a determined effort, he switched his mind to Vlast. He had first met him at a secret anti-communist meeting. Vlast had taken a liking to him. He said Englishmen were always reliable. They had talked. After meeting several times, Vlast had confided to Worthington that at one time he had been a master engraver. He was now working a night shift as an elevator attendant at one of the better hotels. This work gave him his days free. Lowering his voice, he had said that if ever Worthington needed a passport, he should come to him. 'You never know. There is no better man at that game than me.'

At that time Worthington had been very sure of himself, but he had filed this offer away in his mind. He knew there might come a time when he would have to leave Prague and with a false passport.

Up to two weeks ago, things had continued well for Worthington. He had an English Public School appearance and a pleasant manner. He was also an intelligent listener. Every now and then his pupils—professors, politicians, Civil servants—let slip information that he passed to Cain who, in his turn, passed to Dorey. Worthington had watched the dollars grow in his Swiss bank account. Then all of a sudden Malik, a giant with silver coloured hair, had appeared on the scene. Worthington knew this man was the most dangerous agent of the G.R.U., the Soviet Intelligence Service. Worthington had always been aware that he wasn't made of hero material. When he heard that Malik had arrived in Prague, he began immediate preparations to leave. He contacted Vlast. The old man agreed to fake a passport, but he wasn't doing it for nothing. It took Worthington several anxious days to get together enough money by borrowing, dipping into his meagre savings and by persuading some of his more reliable pupils to let him have an advance. During those days, Worthington discovered he was being watched and he guessed Malik suspected him. He also realised another frightening fact. If he were arrested, he would be forced to betray Mala and Cain. The very thought of what Malik's thugs would do to him to extract this betrayal from him sickened him. He knew he would be a babbling, screaming mine of information once in their hands. Dorey would know this. He hated Dorey. He had only met him once and he knew Dorey had distrusted him. Dorey valued Mala and Cain. So what would Dorey do? Sitting on the toilet seat, cigarette smoke staining his thin fingers, Worthington mentally shivered. Dorey would send someone to liquidate him. It was as simple as that. A dead mouth was a silent mouth. So now, he not only had Malik hunting for him, but also one of Dorey's killers.

There came a tap on the bathroom door and then it opened.

'I'm going,' Mala said.

He got hastily off his undignified seat. She was wearing a simple blue dress and he thought she looked lovely. A spasm of desire ran through him. For a long moment he stared at her, then controlling himself, he took an envelope from his breast pocket.

'It's the money for Vlast,' he said, giving the envelope to her. 'For God's sake don't lose it. You have the film and the passport?'

'Yes.' She put the package in her bag and turned to cross the room. His eyes moved down her long, slim back. 'There is something in the fridge if you are hungry.'

'Thank you. Make certain no one is following you.'

She looked sharply at him. She knew that their close association disturbed him and it worried her. She was sure he would control himself, but the sooner he left the better for both of them. He aroused no feelings in her. She just felt embarrassed and uneasy to have him with her.

'I'll watch it,' she said and made for the door.

It took her some twenty minutes to reach Celetna ulice. She began the climb to Vlast's fifth floor apartment. On the third floor, she paused and looked down into the well below. Then satisfied she wasn't being followed, she ran up the other two flights of stairs and rang on Vlast's door bell.

There was a long pause, then the door opened. She was confronted by an enormously fat old man, wearing a grey flannel shirt and stained, black corduroy trousers. The fringe of hair that climbed over his ears was white. His small eyes, button nose and three chins made him a character that Hollywood would have loved.

'Come in,' he said and made a creaking bow. 'I can't remember ever having such a lovely visitor.' He turned and waddled into the small living-room, grey with dust, with two broken-down armchairs, a table and a threadbare carpet. 'I lost my wife.' He slapped dust out of the seat of one of the chairs. 'That's a pretty dress you are wearing. It would be a pity to spoil it.' He lumbered across the room for a copy of *The Morning Sun* and spread it on the seat of the chair. 'There . . . your dress will be quite safe. Please sit down.'

Mala sat down. She took the money, the film cartridge and the passport from her bag. Then she stiffened, staring at the old man's right hand which was heavily bandaged.

'Have you hurt yourself?' she asked.

He looked at his bandaged hand and shrugged.

'It isn't very bad. I cut myself. When you reach my age, cuts can be nasty. Now tell me why I should have so much pleasure.'

'I have come from Mr. Worthington,' she said, trying to control her rising panic. She put the three articles she was holding on the table. 'He said you would do the work quickly.'

Vlast looked at the passport, then shook his head.

'It is unfortunate. Things like this happen . . . always

46

at the wrong time. As soon as my hand has healed, I will of course do it quickly.'

He eyed the envelope. 'Is that the money?' He opened the envelope and counted the notes. Then he nodded, satisfied. 'I like Mr. Worthington. I promised to help him. It won't take long.'

'How long?' Mala asked, tense and wide-eyed.

'A couple of weeks . . . certainly not longer.'

She stared at him and her hands turned into fists.

'But it is now terribly urgent. They are already looking for him!'

Vlast rubbed his unshaven chin. His thick fingers rasped against his stubble and his fat face darkened.

'That is very bad. I'm sorry . . . I can't do it under two weeks. I assure you I would if it were possible.'

Two weeks! Mala was thinking. I can't have him in my room for two weeks!

'Can't you really do it before then?'

'It has to be perfect. If I did it badly, I would be sending him to his death. In two weeks, I should be able to make a perfect job . . . I wouldn't risk it before.'

Mala sat for a long moment in despair, then she got to her feet.

'I'll tell him.'

'Tell him I am very sorry.' The old man's eyes feasted happily on her trim figure. 'Would you like a cup of tea?'

'No . . . no thanks.'

She was already moving to the door. He watched her leave, feeling depressed that someone so attractive, so colourful should be going out of his life. He put the articles she had given him in a drawer and locked it. Then he walked heavily over to the open window and leaned out. He watched her as she walked down the street and until she was out of sight.

Well, Worthington was lucky, he thought, wishing he was forty years younger. He wondered if they were lovers. Sighing, he went back to his dusty armchair and sat down. His bandaged hand was beginning to throb. He would go to the hospital in the afternoon. He must get his hand well so he could keep his promise to Worthington.

* * *

Left on his own, Worthington examined Mala's apartment with care. It consisted of a fair size living-room. A narrow divan bed stood in an alcove. There was a minute kitchenette and a bathroom with a toilet. A range of cupboards stood along one of the walls of the living-room. There was also a small balcony reached by french windows at the far end of the living-room. The balcony, containing two big flowering shrubs in tubs, looked on to a high blank wall of a church. In an emergency, if someone came unexpectedly, Worthington could hide himself on the balcony sure that he wouldn't be seen either from the street nor from the living-room. This gave him a little comfort.

He put his suitcase under the divan bed and then sat down in the armchair. Standing in one of the corners of the living-room was a lifesize, kneeling angel carved from wood . . . a church ornament that someone had found in some antique shop . . . probably the owner of the apartment. He felt more relaxed as he contemplated the angel, admiring the sweep of the wings, the pious expression of the wooden face and the simple robes. It was a masterpiece of carving, he thought. This was something he would like to own. Well, when he finally reached Geneva and got his money, he would look around. He might be lucky enough to find something as good.

He was still thinking about his money and where he would eventually settle once he reached Geneva when he heard someone coming up the stairs. Getting swiftly to his feet, he stepped out on to the balcony, and leaned against the wall, alert and frightened. His fingers touched the butt of his Colt .32 automatic which he carried in a holster under his left armpit. He heard the lock turn and then there was a pause. Cautiously, he peered around the big flowering shrub. He caught a glimpse of Mala as she looked anxiously around the room. He came from behind the shrub.

'Oh!' She caught her breath sharply. 'I—I thought you had gone.'

Worthington smiled bitterly. Her disappointment was so apparent.

48

'No. One must always take precautions. I heard you coming up the stairs.' He paused, looking expectantly at her. 'When will Vlast have my passport ready?'

'He has hurt his hand. He thinks two weeks.'

Blood rushed into Worthington's face, then receded, leaving his face a blotchy white.

'Two weeks? That's ridiculous!'

'I know, but he can't use his hand.' She paused, then said violently, 'You can't stay here for two weeks! You must go! I won't have you here!'

Worthington sat down. Two weeks! Every day and night of those two weeks would be dangerous with Malik hunting for him. There would also be Dorey's killer hunting for him. He felt himself cringe. Leave her? That would be asking for death. This little apartment was his only refuge.

Mala was saying, 'Please go!' Her voice was hysterical. 'I don't want any more to do with you! Don't just sit there . . . take your bag and go!'

Worthington shifted his mind from his troubles to hers. He could understand how she was feeling. How different it would have been if she loved him as he loved her, he thought bitterly. When there is love there is kindness and a willingness to make a sacrifice.

'If I go,' he said quietly, 'they would pick me up quickly. Make no mistake about that. We have already discussed this. I have never been brave . . . few people are really brave. It wouldn't be difficult for them to make me talk. How long do you imagine you would last if they caught me? I must stay here for both our sakes. There is nowhere else for me to go.'

Mala looked at him in despair, realising what he was saying was the truth.

'Then I will go. I'll ask one of my girl friends to put me up.'

'Would that be wise?' Worthington lit a cigarette with an unsteady hand. 'Your friend would want to know why you have left here. Isn't that telling her that I am here?'

She sat down abruptly.

'We can manage,' Worthington went on soothingly.

'You don't leave the club till midnight. I can get all the sleep I need while you are at the club. I promise you I won't be a nuisance.'

She said nothing, but continued to stare down at her hands, tightly clenched in her lap.

Although he loved her, Worthington began to lose patience. Couldn't she show some kindness? Was she so completely indifferent to him?

'I'm trying to be reasonable about this,' he said, an edge to his voice. 'Will you please pull yourself together? Can't you see if they catch me, they will kill both of us?'

She looked up, her face white, her lips trembling.

'Why did you do this to me? I was safe. Why were you so cowardly and selfish as to come here?'

Worthington flinched.

'No one is ever safe,' he said. 'That is a stupid thing to say. I know I am a coward, but you are also cowardly. You are thinking only of yourself. I'm thinking of both of us.' Then as she said nothing, he went on, 'Let us think about lunch. Is there anything to eat? I'm hungry.'

chapter three

Oscar Bruckman had been in Prague now for two days.
He was staying at a modest hotel in the Stare Mesto district, and had been acting like a staid American tourist.
One of the first places of entertainment he had visited was
the Alhambra night club. He had seen Mala Reid's act,
and had noted the time she came on and when her act
finished. Bruckman, who was tone deaf, had no idea if this
attractive girl could sing or not. He didn't care, but he did
appreciate her figure.

He had also been to her apartment block. His keen pho-
tographic eyes had recorded all the necessary details he
would have to use later. He had stepped into the doorway
to light a cigarette. He had noted there was no concierge
nor elevator.

Around five o'clock on this second day of his stay in
Prague he received the green light from Dorey in a coded
cable. Girland had obtained a visa for Prague and would
be leaving the following morning.

As Mala was beginning her act at the Alhambra, Bruckman put the package, containing the thirty thousand dollars Dorey had given him into a shabby brief-case and left
his hotel.

He walked to Mala's apartment. At this time of night,
the streets were practically deserted. Only a few tourists
wandered around, gaping at the beautiful buildings, pausing to examine the various old house signs used before
house numbers came into fashion.

He entered the apartment block and walked casually up
the steep spiral staircase, making no attempt to deaden his

51

footfalls on the bare boards. He was far too astute ever to appear furtive. He climbed the stairs as an expected visitor, and Worthington heard him coming.

The past two days had been a big strain on Worthington. Every sound outside the apartment had sent him scurrying out to the balcony. Mala had been understandably frightened of him, and to his distress she now spent all her waking hours out of the apartment, sitting in cafés, wandering around various museums, going to a movie . . . anything, rather than stay alone with him in the apartment, only returning at eight o'clock when she had to prepare for her act at the Alhambra.

Time hung heavily on Worthington's hands. He had only his uneasy thoughts for company.

Mala had screened the alcove, containing the bed, with a sheet hung over a length of string. On her return from the night club, she would have a few brief, casual words with Worthington, then she would retire behind the screen, leaving Worthington to spend the rest of the bleak hours in an armchair until she again left the apartment early in the morning.

When she was dressing for the night club, Worthington went behind the screen and lay on the bed. He had to listen to her movements, taking a shower and dressing. He wished that she could love him as he loved her. They were two lonely people, he kept telling himself: people hovering on the brink of disaster and certain death. But she gave him no hint of encouragement. She was distant, polite and so obviously anxious to see the last of him.

Now, once again, she had gone to the club, leaving a faint smell of perfume some American admirer had given her lingering in the room and he was faced with four hours of restless sleep on his own. He was about to undress when he heard Bruckman coming up the stairs.

His heart missed a beat. Looking quickly around to make sure he had left no tell-tale sign that he was living in this room, he snapped off the light and tiptoed out on the balcony, easing the french windows shut behind him. He drew his Colt automatic and got behind the flowering shrub. The gun in his hand gave him no confidence. Even in the worse kind of emergency, he couldn't imagine himself ever pulling the trigger.

Bruckman paused outside the front door. The building was silent. He thumbed the door bell and waited. He had his story ready if anyone came to the door. From the mail boxes downstairs, he had taken the name of the owner of the apartment above. He would apologise for his mistake and then walk up the stairs.

He waited patiently, then rang again. After a further wait, he was satisfied the apartment was empty. He took from his wallet a flexible piece of steel and expertly unlocked the door. He moved into the dark room, groped for the light switch and turned it on.

Peering around the shrub, Worthington caught a brief glimpse of Bruckman as he moved into the room. He immediately recognised the big, heavily built man. Fear, he knew was in him, but up to now had never truly experienced, paralysed him.

He knew Bruckman was O'Halloran's strong arm thug who did most of O'Halloran's dirty work. He was an executioner for the C.I.A., used when an Agent with important information threatened to defect.

Who had betrayed him to Bruckman? Worthington wondered, his heart hammering. He thumbed back the safety catch on his gun, but he knew he could never shoot Bruckman. There was this weak, compassionate streak in him that made it impossible for him to take human life. He knelt on the balcony, cold with fear, waiting for Bruckman to discover him.

Minutes passed: nothing happened. Terrified, Worthington again peered into the room.

Bruckman was coming out of the bathroom. He was massively menacing as he looked around the room, then he walked over to the life-size wooden angel and stared thoughtfully at it.

Worthington watched him, puzzled. Bruckman's broad back blocked the angel from Worthington's view. Then Bruckman half-turned and Worthington saw he was holding the angel's wooden head in his hands. This he placed on the floor, then he opened his brief-case and took from

53

it a small package done up in brown paper. He forced the package down the hollow neck of the angel into the body. He worked quickly and without fuss, and in a moment the angel's head had been replaced. He looked around the room, picked up the empty brief-case, walked to the door, turned off the light and closed the door behind him.

Worthington waited, unable to believe his luck, then he gently pushed open the french windows. He could hear Bruckman clumping down the stairs and he moved cautiously across the dark room to the front door. He eased it open. Bruckman's heavy tread was dying away. Then Worthington heard the entrance door slam shut.

He turned on the light and went shakily to the armchair and sat down. He had been too close to death, he thought. He was so badly frightened that he could only sit motionless, staring at the wooden angel, thankful he was still alive. His mind crawled with alarm.

He was still sitting in the chair, now half asleep, his body and mind beginning to relax when Mala returned. As soon as she saw his face, tight with fear and the sweat beads on his forehead, she knew something had happened. Quickly she closed the door and shot the bolt.

'What is it?'

Worthington got slowly to his feet. He made a desperate effort to conceal his fear, but he could see her growing terror.

'Bruckman's been here. He picked the lock. I—I hid on the balcony.'

Mala stared fearfully at him.

'Who is he? What do you mean?'

'He's one of Dorey's men,' Worthington said, trying to control his impatience. 'When I saw him come in, I was sure someone had given me away.' He rubbed his dry lips with the back of his hand. 'I thought he was going to murder me.'

Mala shivered.

'But why should he—he murder you?'

'Dorey knows that if I am caught I will give you and Cain away,' Worthington said, his voice desperate. 'But he wasn't here to kill me.' He pointed to the wooden angel.

54

'He put a package in there. Is that where they leave things for you to pass on?'

'What are you talking about?' Mala stared at the angel. 'He left something in there?'

'Yes. He lifted off the head and put a package in the body. I thought it was something you were expecting . . . after all, you are still working for Dorey.' Seeing how bewildered she looked, he went on, 'If you don't know anything about it, we'd better see what it is.'

'No! Leave it alone! If he left something in there, I don't want to know about it!' Mala exclaimed wildly.

Worthington looked at her in exasperation.

'Are you telling me the truth? Are you sure they don't use that as a hiding place?'

'Of course they don't! Leave it alone! I don't want to know about it!'

'You are behaving like a child. You are an agent. You have already passed a lot of information back to C.I.A. through Cain and me, and you have been paid for doing it. That makes you a professional. Pull yourself together! Sooner or later, they will find a replacement for me. When they do, he will contact you, and you will have to work for him as you have worked for me.'

'I'm not working for them any more!' Mala cried, facing him. 'I've had enough! Will you please go! No one can force me to do what I don't want to do!'

Worthington looked pityingly at her. He could well understand her terror. When he had heard Malik had arrived in Prague, he too had become terrified.

'Please listen to me and don't get so upset,' he said gently. 'You have accepted their money. If they don't want you, they will drop you, but you can never drop them. If you try to drop them they will silence you. The only chance you have of dropping them is to disappear as I am going to disappear. Unless you have a way to get out of this country and hide yourself, then they will kill you.'

She looked desperately at him.

'I don't believe it! They couldn't do that!'

'Why do you imagine I'm leaving Prague? I knew this would happen and I have been preparing for just this emergency.' Worthington paused, hesitated, then went on. 'This is the wrong time to tell you, but I have to.' His weak face was glistening with sweat and his eyes were desperately earnest. 'Mala, I love you. I have been in love with you from the moment we first met. I wish there were less banal words to tell you what you mean to me . . .' He broke off in despair when he saw her shocked expression. 'I shouldn't have told you . . . I am sorry.'

'Sorry?' Her frightened contempt made him shrivel. 'You say you love me? Then why did you come here? Why have you made use of me to save yourself? Love me . . . you mean you love yourself!'

Worthington sat motionless, then finally he said, 'I had nowhere else to go. I hoped and prayed you would have a little feeling for me.'

'I don't want you here!' Mala cried. 'How many more times do I have to tell you? You mean nothing to me! Don't you understand . . . nothing!'

She turned away from him. Worthington studied her long, slim back, thinking how lovely she was, longing to take her in his arms.

'We could go away together,' he said. 'Why don't you come with me to Switzerland? Vlast would fake a passport for you. We could travel as man and wife. When we reach Geneva, you can make up your mind if you would like to stay with me. I have money in Geneva.'

She spun around.

'I'm remaining here! I'm not working for them any more! If only you would go, I'll be safe!'

'No agent is ever safe. If we leave Prague together, you will be safer with me in Geneva.'

'Oh, stop it! Why don't you go!' Her voice shot up a note and Worthington flinched, wondering if the people above or below could hear her.

'We had better see what Bruckman has left here,' he said.

'No! Leave it alone!'

'He could have planted something on you. I don't trust Dorey. He might be betraying you. We must see what it is.'

56

Mala watched in tense silence as he crossed over to the wooden angel and lifted off the head.

* * *

Harry Moss was waiting when Girland got out of the Air Terminal bus at the Departure Centre at Orly Airport. He walked over to Girland as Girland collected his shabby suitcase from the luggage compartment of the bus.

'Hi,' Moss said. 'Here's your ticket. Let's get rid of your bag and then we'll talk.'

Having checked in and got rid of his suitcase, Girland walked with Moss over to an empty bench and sat down.

From his cowboy shirt pocket, Moss took a folded piece of paper.

'Here's the address. The money is in the body of a wooden angel.' He had received this information from Dorey the previous evening who had, in turn, received it from Bruckman in a coded telegram from Prague. 'It's dead easy. The head lifts off. You're booked to return in three days . . . Saturday. I'll be right here, waiting for you.'

'That is one thing I'll bet on,' Girland said dryly. He read the address which meant nothing to him. 'A wooden angel?'

'Yeah. It stands in the left hand corner of the room. You can't miss it.'

'Is anyone living in the apartment?' Girland asked, putting the address in his wallet.

'I wouldn't know . . . could be. Accommodation in Prague is tight, but that's up to you.' Moss gave him a sly look. 'You can't expect to pick up all that dough without earning it, can you?'

'What else can you tell me about the place?'

'There's no concierge. It's a walk-up . . . fourth floor. The lock on the door is nothing.' Moss was quoting from the information Dorey had given him. 'All you have to watch out for is that no one is in the apartment when you break in.'

Girland rubbed the back of his neck while he thought.

57

Then he shrugged. This job worried him a little. It seemed too glib, but he kept telling himself he had nothing to lose.

'I have the address . . . where's the spending money?'

Reluctantly, Moss produced a small roll of notes.

'Here you are . . . a thousand francs. This will just about skin me . . . don't waste it.'

Girland put the notes in his wallet as a voice, over the public address system, announced that passengers on Flight 714 to Prague should now proceed to Gate No. 8.

'Well, here I go,' he said, getting to his feet. 'Don't have a haemorrhage if you don't see me Saturday. This could be trickier than you think.'

'There's nothing to it.' Moss walked with Girland to the escalator that would take him to Gate 8. 'I'll be right here . . . Saturday.'

Girland had his boarding card punched, then with a wave of his hand, he ran up the moving staircase.

Fifteen minutes later, he was climbing the tourist class stairway into the Caravelle. The air hostess fluttered her eyelids at him and Girland gave her his charming smile. As long as he could remember, he had always been the darling of air hostesses. It came as no surprise, after the plane had taken off that the air hostess came down the aisle and whispered to him that there was plenty of room in the first class compartment.

Girland regarded her. She was a pretty little thing with sparkling dark eyes and a saucy smile.

'Well, that's nice,' he said and leaving his cramped seat, followed by disapproving eyes, he made his way to the first class compartment.

He refused champagne and chose a double Scotch on the rocks. He flirted for a while with the air hostess, then when she had gone, and now slightly mellowed by his drink, he relaxed back in his seat and did some thinking.

Bruckman's mysterious visit to his apartment still bothered him. During the two days he had been waiting for the Prague visa, he had gone over his apartment with skill and care. He had wondered if Dorey had wanted to bug the apartment, but he found no bug. Had Dorey planted something on him? Again he found nothing suspicious. Why should Dorey want to plant something on him anyway? He finally decided that Dorey was still hoping to get some of the money back Girland had taken off him, but although this seemed unlikely, Girland couldn't think of any other explanation for Bruckman's visit.

Harry Moss worried him too. Although Girland had checked Moss's story, it still seemed a little far-fetched and Moss seemed to Girland too much like a character out of a B movie.

Girland shrugged impatiently. Well, he would see what happened when he reached Prague. At this moment the air hostess was bringing him caviare on toast. As there were only two other passengers in the first class compartment, she sat by his side. They flirted, chatted and ate while the plane carried them over the Iron Curtain and to the Prague airport.

As soon as Harry Moss saw the Caravelle airborne, he hurried to a telephone booth and called Dorey.

'He's off,' he said. 'Hook, line and sinker. Is there anything else you want me to do?'

'No, there's nothing else,' Dorey said. 'Good work, Alan. I'm sending you a small contribution. Thank you very much.'

'Don't mention it. It was a pleasure.' There was a pause, then Moss said, 'Don't make that contribution too small, Uncle.'

Dorey grimaced, then hung up. He scribbled a telegram to Bruckman, alerting him of the time of Girland's arrival. He added this warning: 'Girland knows you. Keep well out of sight and don't under-estimate him. This operation must work.'

He gave the telegram to his secretary, Mavis Paul. When she had gone, he sat back in his chair and lit a cigarette.

He felt pleased with himself.

* * *

Three men sat around a table in a large airless room of the Ministry of the Interior. In this vast building, built like

59

a fortress, the Prague Secret Police had their headquarters.

Suk, second in charge of the Secret Police, was staring at a large scale street map of the City, spread out on the table. There was a strip of plaster on his bald head, covering the cut and the bruise from Worthington's attack. A throbbing headache still tormented him.

Opposite him, Malik sat like a massive Sphinx, his cold green eyes moving from Suk to the map and then back to Suk. The third man was Boris Smernoff, thickset with a dark, cruel face and a bald patch which he tried vainly to hide by combing long thin strands of black hair over the ever expanding baldness. He was Malik's right hand man, an expert shot and G.R.U.'s most persistent and successful hunter of men.

'He can't escape,' Suk said. 'He must be somewhere here,' and he tapped the street map. 'It is only a matter of time.'

'You don't think time is important?' Malik said in his clipped English, the common language between these two men. 'It is only a matter of time? You have been negligent, Comrade. I warned you about this man. Now, he has disappeared. You say it is only a matter of time. I hope so. What steps are you taking to find him?'

Suk wiped the sweat off his forehead. Without looking at Malik, he said, 'He can't get out of the country. I'm sure of that. We are now making inquiries. Someone must be hiding him. We have already checked all the hotels. The airport and the frontier posts have been alerted. We . . .'

Malik silenced him with an impatient wave of his hand.

'When you find him I want to talk to him . . . understand?'

'Yes, Comrade Malik.'

'What is more important is his replacement. They are certain to replace him. I want details of everyone coming by air, train and road. I don't think Dorey will send in anyone just yet, but he may. Anyone slightly suspect must be doubly screened. Do you understand?'

'Yes, Comrade Malik.'

'Well, get on with it and find Worthington.'

Suk got to his feet and left the office, closing the door softly behind him.

Malik looked at Smernoff who was lighting a cigarette. 'Well? What is it?'

Smernoff smiled, showing his tobacco-stained teeth.

'This man Jonathan Cain,' he said. 'He is possibly of interest: a buyer of glass. He comes to Prague twice a month. He had lunch with Dorey four days ago. The report came through as routine from one of the waiters at Chez Joseph, a luxury Paris restaurant with private rooms. Dorey and Cain met . . . that's for certain. Malinkov merely mentioned it in his weekly report. He said it might mean nothing. Dorey often lunches with various friends.'

'Malinkov is a fool,' Malik said. 'What do you know about Cain?'

'Very little . . . he is a typical American business man.. When he comes here, he frequently visits the Alhambra night club. There is nothing against him in any way . . . except he lunched with Dorey.'

Malik leaned back in his chair, frowning.

'The Alhambra night club? Do you know it?'

'I've been there.' Smernoff flicked ash on the floor. 'You can eat reasonably well there. They have small booths where you can be alone. The acts are noisy and not much, but there is a girl singer whose parents were American and Czech. The father was against the régime . . . he was executed. The girl calls herself Mala Reid . . . she's taken her mother's name.'

Malik examined his blunt fingernails, then glanced up.

'Has Cain had anything to do with her?'

'He seems to be an admirer of hers. Several times he has given her flowers. He has never gone with her to her apartment.'

'Flowers . . .' Malik thought, then stretched his long, massive arms. 'Yes . . . perhaps we might take a look at this girl, Boris. Have her watched. This could be a waste of time, but at the moment, we seem to have nothing else to use except time.' He looked up; his green eyes glittering. 'I want to know everything about this girl . . . understand?'

Smernoff got to his feet.

'So do I,' he said and left the room.

Malik stood up and walked over to the window. There were two pigeons on the lower balcony. The male was going through his elaborate dance of love. The female was ignoring him. Malik watched them for some moments. He felt contempt for the male pigeon. What a fool the male was when he became infatuated with the female, he thought and turned away.

He began to think about Cain . . . then his mind switched to Worthington and his possible replacement. Perhaps, after all, Suk was right. In this country, it could only be a matter of time, and, of course, patience.

* * *

Worthington fingered the brown paper packet he had taken from the angel's body.

'You see? This is a plant,' he said. 'I never trusted Dorey.'

Mala made no attempt to hide her terror.

'But why? What have I done?'

Worthington shrugged.

'How can we tell? We must see what he has planted on you,' and he took from his pocket a penknife.

'We'd better not . . .'

'Of course we must, then we are prepared.' Sitting at the table Worthington began to slide the blade of the knife carefully under the Sellotape that secured the parcel. It took him some minutes to open it. Mala stood over him, watching, her heart beating wildly.

Worthington unwrapped the paper and drew out the thick packet of one hundred dollar bills.

They both stared unbelievingly at the money, then with shaking fingers, Worthington began to count the bills.

After a long tense silence, he said, 'For God's sake! This is a fortune! Thirty thousand dollars!'

Mala turned cold. She sat down abruptly by his side.

'What does it mean?'

Worthington stared at the money on the table for some

time, then he suddenly nodded. 'There can only be one explanation. This isn't a plant, Mala. This is funds for my replacement.' His thin face darkened. 'They never gave me money like this. I warned you . . . when this man replaces me, he will contact you. This is why Bruckman hid the money here. The money is to buy information.' He sat back. 'They have already written me off. My replacement will come here and collect the money. They are using your place to finance him. They don't give a damn about the risk to you.'

Mala drew in a shuddering breath.

'All that money!'

'They have no right to do this!' Worthington went on. The sight of the hundred dollar bills fascinated him. 'If they had consulted you . . . you could have refused or agreed, but that's not the way they work. They do it like this . . . not caring what happens to you.' He leaned forward, tapping the dollar bills. 'Malik might come here and find these . . . then you would be done for.'

Mala also was hypnotised by the sight of so much money.

'What are we going to do?'

'With this money,' Worthington said quietly and emphatically, 'you will have no trouble leaving Prague. You will be independent. You could come with me to Geneva. You could buy a passport . . . it's a fortune!'

Mala shifted her eyes from the money to him.

'But it doesn't belong to me! I couldn't use it for myself!'

'They haven't thought of you . . . why should you think of them? Money means nothing to them. If we take this, they will replace it. This money can buy your freedom.'

Mala hesitated, then shook her head.

'No! Put it back . . . I'm not touching it.'

Worthington regarded her, then seeing the determined expression in her eyes, he shrugged wearily.

'All right . . . you are being stupid, but if you really feel like that I can't help you.'

She pressed her hands to her face.

63

'Yes, I feel like that.' She got to her feet. 'Please put it back where you found it.' She again looked at the money, then she walked slowly over to the screen. 'I'm going to bed.' She paused and looked directly at him. 'All right, I know I am stupid, but I'm not a thief!'

'When one's life is in balance,' Worthington said quietly, 'I suppose it could be said it is better to be a thief than to be stupid.'

She hesitated, then went behind the sheet. Worthington heard her drop on the bed. He looked at the money. With thirty thousand dollars, plus his Swiss savings, he would be safe for life, he thought. He didn't hesitate for more than a moment or so. Getting to his feet, he went into the kitchenette and returned with two copies of *The Morning Sun*. He folded the newspapers to the size of the hundred dollar bills. Then he put the folded newspapers into the wrapping and began to reseal the packet.

'What are you doing?' Mala asked, appearing from behind the screen. 'What do you think you are doing?'

'Not being stupid.' Worthington satisfied himself the packet was secure, then got up and crossed to the wooden angel. He forced the packet down the hollow neck into the body. He replaced the head. 'You can be as stupid as you like, but I know the value of money.'

'You mean you're taking it? You can't! It doesn't belong to you!'

Worthington picked up the packet of money.

'Go to bed. You're tired. You must leave this to me.'

'What do you plan to do with it?'

'It's better for you to know nothing about it. Please go to bed.'

'We could never smuggle it out. It's you who is being stupid!'

Worthington looked at her, his expression resigned.

'I am doing my best to get you out of a mess. You don't seem to realise what a damn awful mess you are in. Dorey's replacement mustn't find this money here. You must not be implicated. Since you are so honest, will you please leave me to look after your interests?'

She saw the sincere, anxious expression in his eyes and the tension on his weak face.

She hesitated, then asked, 'Where will you hide it?'

, He drew in a long breath of relief. So, in spite of her honesty, she was at last realising not only her danger, but what this money could mean to them both.

'Under the angel. We can get at it quickly if we have to. I'll tape it to the base of the angel.'

'All right.' She came to him, her cold fingers touching his wrist. 'I'm sorry, Alec. I don't mean to be difficult. I do understand how you feel about me. If you think we can do it, I will come with you to Switzerland.'

Worthington smiled wryly. It was the money, of course, he thought, not himself that now made her change her mind.

'You must see Vlast tomorrow. Tell him you need a British passport. He'll get you one if the money is there.' Worthington turned the packet in his hands. 'Have you an envelope to take this?'

'There's a plastic bag in the kitchen . . . would that do?'

'That would do.'

She saw the sad, disillusioned expression on his face and she felt ashamed.

'Thank you, Alec. I can't help it if I don't love you, can I? I'm sorry about the way I've treated you . . . I'm just scared stiff.'

Worthington smiled at her.

'That's all right. I'm scared stiff too. We'll make it, Mala. Once you are in Geneva, you may see things differently. You never know . . . you might even come to like me.'

While they were talking two thick-set men, wearing black mackintoshes and black slouch hats took over a room that overlooked Mala's apartment on the opposite side of the street. An elderly woman who had lived in this room for many years was ruthlessly bundled out to stay in an old people's home.

Smernoff had given his orders. From the moment the

65

two men took up their positions behind the lace curtains of the window, Mala was under the G.R.U.'s microscope.

* * *

Mavis Paul, Dorey's secretary, dark, beautifully built and very assured, glanced up as O'Halloran came into her office.

'Good morning, Captain,' she said and gave him her bright smile she reserved for her favourites. 'He is expecting you . . . go right on in.'

O'Halloran grinned, giving her a dashing salute.

'You look pretty good this morning,' he said gallantly. 'Come to think of it, when don't you look good?'

She laughed.

'I've heard that story dozens of times. Anyway, thanks,' and she flicked a finger at Dorey's office door. 'Right in there, Captain,' and she began to hammer away at her I.B.M. electric typewriter.

O'Halloran pulled a resigned face.

'I've nothing to do tonight,' he said. 'How about a gorgeous dinner at Lasserre? Three stars and a sliding roof? Interest you?'

'My roof doesn't slide,' she said, pausing for a brief moment. 'No dates . . . but thanks,' and she continued to type.

'Well, I guess a guy can always try,' O'Halloran said and walked over to Dorey's office door. 'Take a raincheck on it.'

'I will and thank you.'

But he knew she wouldn't. He had come to realise that Mavis Paul not only took her work seriously, but also her after working hours. She just did not make dates.

He tapped on the door and entered.

As usual, Dorey was immersed in a file. He glanced up, waved to a chair and went on reading.

O'Halloran sat down and put his service cap on the floor by his side. A minute later, Dorey signed the file and pushed it out of his way. He sat back and smiled at O'Halloran.

66

'Glad to see you back, Tim. Had a good trip?'

O'Halloran had been to Antwerp on a dull and unprofitable assignment. This had kept him out of Paris for the past three days.

'Okay . . . nothing much,' he said. 'You'll get my report tomorrow.'

'Things go well this end,' Dorey said with satisfaction. 'I've had confirmation from Bruckman that Girland has arrived in Prague. Latimer is waiting to fly in. This has to be carefully timed. The moment Girland's picked up, Latimer goes in. I have an open reservation for him so there'll be no delay. Probably in a couple of days, Latimer will be in Prague. Girland works fast. He'll grab the money and then try to get out. Bruckman is covering him all the time.'

'Anyone else out there?' O'Halloran asked. 'It's throwing a lot on Bruckman.'

'He can handle it. I asked him if he wanted help, but he said no. I have a lot of confidence in him.'

O'Halloran looked dubious.

'Yeah. I'd have thought he should have had help. Girland is tricky. If he once gets the idea that Bruckman is tailing him, I don't think Bruckman stands a chance.'

Dorey shifted impatiently.

'The trouble with you, Tim, is you are a pessimist. Bruckman knows his job. He'll keep out of sight.'

O'Halloran lifted his heavy shoulders.

'I'd be happier if he had someone with him.'

'You can leave this to me,' Dorey said. He was pleased with his arrangements and he wasn't going to listen to any criticism from O'Halloran. 'By the way, there's a memo from the Joint Chiefs of Staff that came in last week while you were away. It's so Top Secret I can't let it out of my office.' He got to his feet and crossed over to his safe. 'It covers our future planning in Vietnam and how we are to cope with any possible Russian interference. It's pure dynamite! I hope they know what they are doing. Anyway L.B.J. has initialled it, so I suppose they do. There's a paragraph about our security out there you should see.'

He spun the dial, pressed a combination of buttons and then opened the safe. After a moment, he came back with a long white envelope with a red sticker on it. He handed the envelope to O'Halloran.

'Read it, Tim. It'll make your hair stand on end. I've another goddamn file to get off.'

He sat down at his desk and pulled a file towards him while O'Halloran lifted the flap of the envelope and took out two sheets of paper.

There was a moment's pause, then O'Halloran said, 'What's this? I guess you've given me the wrong envelope.'

Dorey wrenched his mind away from the file he was studying and frowned at O'Halloran.

'What's that?'

O'Halloran offered him the two sheets of paper.

'This isn't anything from the Joint Chiefs of Staff. This is a key to a code we scrapped last month.'

'What the hell are you talking about?' Dorey said, stiffening. He snatched the sheets of paper from O'Halloran and stared at them.

Watching, O'Halloran saw the blood drain out of Dorey's face. The sheets of paper fluttered onto Dorey's desk. He looked so bad, so white that O'Halloran started to his feet.

Jeepers! he thought. He's having a heart attack.

'What is it, Chief?' he asked sharply. 'Want me to get help?'

Dorey made an effort. Slowly, he gained control of himself and then he glared at O'Halloran, fury sparking in his eyes.

'Shut up! Let me think!' His voice was cold and rasping.

O'Halloran recognised the danger signals. It was seldom he had seen Dorey in this mood. He sat down and waited, not looking at Dorey.

Dorey again picked up the two sheets of paper and examined them, then he reached across the desk and picked up the envelope which he also examined. He dropped it on his blotter and pushing back his chair, he walked over to the safe. O'Halloran watched him check through the contents, then Dorey turned. His white face was drawn and old looking, but his mouth was hard and firm and his eyes glittering.

'Tim . . . I've done something inexcusable.' He walked slowly to his chair and sat down. 'Those papers I imagined I had given to Bruckman to put in Girland's suitcase . . . I put them in a Top Secret envelope to impress the Czechs. I had the Chiefs of Staff memo on my desk when Bruckman came in. Somehow . . . I must have been incredibly careless . . . I gave him the wrong envelope.' He paused, staring down at his hands. 'So Girland of all people has taken a Tops memo into Prague of all places! If the Russians get hold of it, all hell could explode and I'm finished!'

O'Halloran stared at Dorey for a moment stunned, unable to believe he had heard aright, then seeing Dorey's expression, he knew it must be right. At once he became the cold, alert thinking machine whose reputation for swift, shrewd action had won him his place in the Security Division.

'I'll cable Bruckman,' he said crisply. 'He'll get the envelope. Girland can't possibly get the money and leave Prague for two or three days. We'll cancel the operation. If Bruckman doesn't alert the Czech police that Girland has this money, they won't stop him when he leaves, so we have two covers. Even if Bruckman fails to get the envelope, the Czech police won't stop Girland leaving if they know nothing about the money. Right?'

'There's Malik,' Dorey said quietly. 'He could stop Girland.'

'Then Bruckman must get the envelope,' O'Halloran said.

'Do you think he is capable of handling this? My God! You were right, Tim. I should have sent someone with him. This is now a hell of an assignment for him to handle alone.'

'He's a good man. He's damn well got to handle it! There's no time to send anyone else to help him.'

Dorey hesitated, then nodded. He drew a sheet of paper towards him and began to write a cable to Bruckman. Watching his steady hand as he wrote, O'Halloran shook his head in silent admiration. Here was a man on the brink of disaster whose slip might turn the Cold War into a Hot War and whose career could come to an abrupt end but who was now in complete control of himself and right back in the fight to save the situation.

'Think this will do?' Dorey said, handing O'Halloran his draft cable.

O'Halloran read it. It's urgency was unmistakable.

'Yes. Do you want me to encode it?'

The two men looked at each other, then Dorey nodded.

'I'd be glad, Tim. Let's try to keep this between our-selves as long as we can. If Bruckman fails to get the memo back, I'll have to alert Washington.' Dorey stared bleakly into space. 'If I have to do that, I might just as well cut my throat.'

O'Halloran snorted, then picking up the draft cable and snatching his cap, he left the office for the Code and Cipher Division.

Mavis Paul paused in her typing as O'Halloran swept past her. She was startled. She looked anxiously at Dorey's office door. What had gone wrong? she wondered. O'Halloran must have something bad on his mind not to have paused to say good-bye to her.

chapter four

Bruckman had never taken Girland seriously. He regarded him merely as a layabout who had had a lot of luck when he had worked for the C.I.A. He knew him to be quick with a gun, an expert karate fighter, but also a womaniser, and this was something Bruckman could never forgive. He considered O'Halloran's respect for Girland's abilities grossly exaggerated. Since he regarded Girland with contempt, he didn't take the precautions he would have done had he been convinced that Girland was a true professional and here, he made a fatal mistake.

Girland spotted him as Girland was registering at the Alcron Hotel. He caught a brief glimpse of Bruckman in a mirror behind the desk as he was completing the registration card. Bruckman was moving quickly to the small bar at the other end of the lobby. Girland immediately recognised him.

Girland completed the form, his brain alerting into top gear.

Bruckman!

As soon as he had reached his bedroom on the third floor and had got rid of the porter who had carried up his suitcase, Girland dropped into an easy chair, lit a cigarette and for some minutes appraised the situation.

Why was Bruckman in Prague? Why should he be at the Alcron Hotel? Was there a connection between his breaking into Girland's Paris apartment and now being in Prague?

Girland mulled this over in his mind and then, suddenly, the nickel dropped.

71

Good grief! he thought. Of course! I should have tumbled to it when that kid in the stretch pants told me Bruckman had broken in. Boy! Am I slipping! I wondered if the big slob was planting something on me. I checked but I didn't check deep enough. He did plant something and he's planted it in my suitcase! Whatever it is, I've brought it behind the Iron Curtain!

He got out of the chair, picked up his suitcase and tossed the contents onto the bed. He examined the empty suitcase carefully, but could see nothing suspicious. Taking out a penknife, he made a cut in the lining, then ripped the lining out of the case. Neatly Sellotaped to the bottom of the case was a white envelope with a red sticker on it.

Girland let out a hissing breath. He knew this particular sticker indicated that the contents of the envelope was Top Secret. Carefully, he eased the envelope free, then laying it on the dressing table, he spent some minutes levering the flap open with the penknife. He removed two flimsy sheets of paper from the envelope, then he sat down.

He read the contents three times. He examined the President's initials which he had seen often enough to recognise. He stared at the typed heading:

From the Joint Chiefs of Staff. Tops Only.

and the brief distribution:

> *For Secstate.*
> *For All Ambassadors.*
> *For C.I.A. Divisional Head Only. (Copy 22).*

What the hell goes on? he thought. If this is a plant for the Soviets to get hold of, it could start a third world war! Just what the hell is this?

He read the memo for a fourth time, then lit a cigarette and stared into space, his brain busy.

Although he was now no longer an active agent, he hadn't forgotten his training and he had a sound political background. He was certain that the Joint Chiefs of Staff hadn't intended that this explosive document should be

72

taken behind the Iron Curtain. This much was obvious. Somewhere, along the line, someone—possibly Dorey—had slipped up. Or could it be that Dorey had become a double agent and he was using Girland to take this document out of Paris?

Girland decided against this idea. It was unthinkable. But it might be that Bruckman was a double agent. Again Girland dismissed the idea. If the document had been a photo-copy, Bruckman could be a suspect. But this was a numbered, original copy and it would be quickly missed. The obvious explanation was that Dorey—if it was Dorey—had slipped up.

Why should I care? Girland asked himself. I've been used as a sucker. I bet there's no stolen payroll, no wooden angel. This is some bright scheme, dreamed up by Dorey, that has turned sour. But what's it all about?

He sat for some time thinking, but he could think of no explanation. Looking again at the two sheets of paper, he wondered what to do with them. His first reaction was to burn them, then he realised if he did so, Dorey's career would be finished. Play this cool, he told himself. You could still come out of Prague with a profit. Right now I have Dorey over a barrel. This is a matter of negotiation. Dorey has made use of me. Now it is my turn to make use of him.

He put the two sheets of paper back in the envelope, then getting to his feet, he crossed to the dressing table. He removed the centre drawer. Kneeling, he fixed the envelope to the top of the space left by removing the drawer. This wasn't the safest place to hide such a dangerous document, but he was confident that as a temporary hiding place it would do. He replaced the drawer.

It was now half-past one and he went thoughtfully down to the restaurant where he had a good lunch of hors d'oeuvres, lamb chops and fruit salad.

After lunch, he went over to the boutique that sold souvenirs of Prague and bought a street guide. He sat in the lounge and studied the map of the city, locating Chivatova ulice, the address Harry Moss had given him. He found it was within walking distance of the hotel and decided he would take a look at the street.

Leaving the hotel, he walked down to the main street with its clanging trams and swarms of people, moving around like a disturbed ant's nest. It would be dead easy, he thought for Bruckman to tail me in this mob and he paused every now and then to look into shop windows, turning to scan the people scurrying around him, but failing to see Bruckman.

He had no need to worry about Bruckman. At this moment, Bruckman had returned to his own hotel, satisfied he now knew where Girland was staying and sure Girland wouldn't make an attempt to collect the money until he had cased Mala Reid's apartment block. The attempt, Bruckman told himself, would take place the following day.

When Bruckman asked for his room key, the clerk handed him the key and a telegram. Up in his shabby room, Bruckman read the telegram. It was a request for certain missing invoices, followed by a list of numbers and letters. These, Bruckman knew, were the real guts of the message in code.

Twenty minutes later, he had decoded the message which now ran:

Ult. Urg. Grl. Pa.s.c. Im Rt. T.S. Ay dl. Liq i.n. Rt. a.a.c.rpt. a.c. vt. D.

Translated, this told Bruckman:

Ultimate urgency. Papers in Girland's suitcase must be returned immediately. They are Top Secret. Make any deal with him. If necessary, liquidate him. Return these papers at any cost, repeat at any cost. Vital. Dorey.

Bruckman re-read the message, then sitting back in his chair, he blew out his cheeks. Just what the hell is this? he thought. Again he read the message. The sense of urgency infected him and he got to his feet. He had his orders. It

74

shouldn't be difficult to get the papers back. Girland had no idea they were in his suitcase. He set fire to Dorey's cable and to the decoded message and let the ashes drop in the ashtray. Then he unlocked his brief-case that was lying on the desk and took from it a .32 police automatic. He checked the magazine, then slid the gun into his pocket. Again from the brief-case he took a black three inch silencer which he also dropped into his pocket. *If necessary, liquidate him.* He would rather knock Girland off than try to make a deal with him. Girland was too tricky to make a deal with, Bruckman thought as he moved heavily from his room.

His hotel was five minutes walking distance from the Alcron Hotel. He reached the Alcron at twenty minutes past three. The American tourists who infested the big luxury hotel were out, sightseeing. There was a quiet calm in the lobby and the lounge. Bruckman walked over to the Head Porter's desk.

The Head Porter gave him a little nod and looked expectantly at him.

'You have Mr. Girland here?' Bruckman asked.

The Hall Porter consulted his register.

'Yes, sir. Room 347.' He turned and looked at the key rack. 'Mr. Girland is out right now. Do you wish to leave a message?'

'That's okay,' Bruckman said. 'I'll telephone him. Thanks.'

He wandered over to the Boutique shop and looked at the souvenir gifts, then when he was sure the Hall Porter had forgotten him, he walked over to the elevators.

'Floor three,' he said.

As he walked down the long corridor, checking the room numbers, he thought that this was a dead easy assignment. With Girland out, he could collect the papers and then telegram Dorey for instructions.

He had his flexible steel pick in his hand as he reached the door of room 347. The corridor was deserted. In ten seconds, Bruckman had unlocked the door and entered the bedroom. He looked around, his heavy red face disapproving. This punk knows how to live, he thought, remembering his own tiny, shabby hotel room. He shut the door and slid the bolt. Then he walked over to Girland's suitcase that was on the luggage rack. He opened it, relieved to find it wasn't locked, then he had a rush of blood to his head. The lining had been ripped out . . . the suitcase was empty.

Bruckman stood staring down into the empty suitcase and he cursed under his breath. How the hell had this goddamn layabout found out about the papers? Well, he had! Bruckman dropped the lid of the suitcase and looked around the room:

He knew it would be a waste of time to search the room. Girland was a trained agent. He had either taken the document with him or had hidden it so securely that Bruckman would have to take the room apart to find it. If he did this, the fact would be reported, and the Security Police would move in. This was something Bruckman wanted to avoid at all cost.

He took out his gun and screwed on the silencer. He had now to talk Girland into making a deal. Obviously, Girland would have read the document, so even if he parted with it, he could still be in a position to blackmail Dorey. Bruckman rubbed his fleshy jaw. He could promise him anything. Girland was only interested in money. So he would agree to pay any sum Girland asked for. Then once Girland parted with the document, he would kill him. One well directed silent shot and Bruckman could walk out of the hotel, get on the next plane to Paris and his assignment was finished.

Pleased with his thinking, Bruckman crossed the room and slid back the bolt, then sat down in the easy chair. He had his silenced gun under his fat thigh, lit a cigarette and prepared himself for Girland's return.

While Bruckman was waiting, Girland had reached Chivatova ulice. He was now satisfied no one was following him. Away from the main streets and once in the narrow lanes that branched like veins off the busy thoroughfares, he could be sure he wasn't being tailed. He found the apartment block he was looking for and he paused outside the high doorway that led to a dark, dirty lobby. He

76

looked to right and left, then certain no one was watching, he moved into the lobby. A line of mail boxes on the shabby paint peeling wall told him that Mala Reid occupied an apartment on the fifth floor which Harry Moss had said had been his hide-out.

He climbed the stairs and finally reached the front door on which was pinned a card which read: *Mala Reid*.

Girland thumbed the bell push, moved back and waited. There was a long pause, then as he was about to ring again, the door opened.

He regarded the sabled haired girl with unexpected pleasure. Quite a doll! he thought and turned on his charming smile. His eyes ran over her. She was wearing a light blue sleeveless frock that clung to her figure with the caress of a well fitting glove.

'Excuse me,' he said. 'Do you happen to speak English?'

Mala had been preparing to visit Vlast again. She had been to his apartment in the morning, only to find him out. The sight of this tall, broad shouldered American made her heart skip a beat.

'Yes,' she said, her voice a little shrill. 'What is it?'

Girland looked beyond her into the big living-room. He saw the wooden angel in the corner. Well, at least, that part of Harry Moss's story was true.

'Would Harry Moss live here?' he asked, wondering why the girl was so obviously frightened.

'No.'

'Well, heck!' Girland looked rueful. 'That's too bad. He gave me this address. I've come all the way from New York . . . he's an old friend of mine. Would you know where he's got to?'

'No,' Mala said, 'I can't help you,' and she closed the door in his face.

Girland hesitated. Don't push your luck too far, he told himself. At least there's a wooden angel. This needs thinking about and careful handling. He turned and walked down the stairs to the street. Who was Mala Reid? A nice dish, he thought. What made her so scared? He paused outside the building while he thought. Could it be the money was really inside that angel? If it was, how could he get at it? He would have to find out when the girl left the apartment and if she lived alone. Did she know the money was there? Girland shook his head. It wasn't going to be easy, but if it meant picking up thirty thousand dollars, he couldn't expect it to be easy.

It was while he stood in the sunshine, outside the building that Zerov, one of the men Smernoff had planted in the opposite building, photographed him. It was a routine picture. Everyone entering and leaving the opposite apartment block was photographed. Zerov had already taken thirty-five pictures and he now wound off the film which he passed to his companion Nicalok.

'Get it processed,' he said. 'Comrade Smernoff will be expecting something from us.'

Nicalok took the film cartridge and left the apartment. By then, Girland was walking back to the Alcron, pondering how he could find out more about Mala Reid. As he walked up the main street, leading to his hotel, he came upon an arcade, leading to the entrance of the Alhambra night club. He was passing it when he came to an abrupt stop. On a bill posted to the wall was Mala Reid's name and a photograph of her, wearing black tights and a bra. The Czech letter press meant nothing to him, but the photograph was all he wanted. So . . . He moved on. Well, he now knew where she worked. Tonight, he would go to the Alhambra. He reached the hotel and asked for his key. The Hall Porter handed it to him.

'There was a gentleman inquiring for you, sir,' he said. 'He said he would telephone later.'

'Is that right?' Girland was puzzled. 'I can't imagine who it would be. Do you remember him?'

'Yes, sir.' The Hall Porter was proud of his memory. 'A tall, heavily built gentleman. He has had an accident to his right ear.'

Girland grinned.

'Oh, sure. I didn't know he was here. He's an old friend of mine. Thanks.' He slid a pack of Pall Mall cigarettes across the desk. He had quickly discovered that cigarettes were much more appreciated in Prague than money.

He rode up in the elevator. So Bruckman was asking for

him, he thought. Watch it, he told himself. This could be action stations.

He reached his bedroom door, unlocked it and swung the door open. Then he walked in. The sight of Bruckman sitting in the easy chair came as no surprise. He was glad he had been tipped off by the Hall Porter.

'Hello, Oscar, nice to see you again,' he said, moving into the room and closing the door. 'How's the wife and kids?'

Bruckman stubbed out his cigarette in an ash tray that was now overflowing with cigarette butts. He shifted his weight slightly so he could get at his gun. His red, fleshy face was expressionless, his cold, grey eyes never left Girland.

'Sit down, punk,' he said in his cop voice. 'You and me have to talk.'

Girland smiled at him.

'Now, Oscar, try to act your age,' he said, leaning against the door. 'You're getting a little long in the tooth for that kind of talk and you've put on too much weight. With that fat belly you're carrying around like a pregnant cow and all the booze you have been swilling, you're not in my class. Do you want to start something? It would be a pleasure. Where's your buddy boy, O'Brien? Remember what I did to him the last time you tried to get tough?'

Bruckman produced his gun. He was still lightning fast and the gun jumped into his hand in one dazzling movement.

'I said sit down, punk!' he said, with a snarl in his voice.

Girland laughed.

'Oscar, you slay me. You should be on the movies . . . strictly B features, but you might make quite a decent living. Go ahead and shoot me.' He walked deliberately up to Bruckman. When he was close to the big man, he looked down at him, still smiling. 'Go on, Oscar. Fire away,' then the side of his hand smashed down on Bruckman's wrist, sending the gun flying across the room.

Bruckman cursed and started to his feet, but Girland shoved him back in the chair.

'Relax, Oscar. You can't murder me just yet. We have to talk . . . remember?'

Bruckman nursed his wrist. His eyes glowered hate at Girland who walked over to the bed and dropped on to it. He stretched out, folding his hands behind his head.

'Go ahead, Oscar,' he said, staring up at the ceiling. 'What's on the thing you call your mind?'

Bruckman continued to massage his wrist, then at last, getting some feeling back into it, he got up and picked up his gun. He put it on the table near him, then sat down again.

Glaring at Girland, he said, 'You know . . . you have a T.S., Girland. I want it.'

'You want it?' Girland grinned. 'What an understatement! I'll tell you who also wants it: Mr. Johnson wants it. Mr. Kosygin wants it. Mr. Ho Chi Minh wants it . . . and more than any of them, my dear old pal Dorey wants it.'

Bruckman contained his fury with an effort that turned his face dark.

'Let's have it, Girland, and let's cut out the funny talk.'

Girland raised his head, his eyebrows lifting.

'I wouldn't have thought any of this funny, Oscar,' he said. 'Suppose we begin at the beginning. You broke into my Paris apartment and planted this T.S. in my suitcase. I can only imagine you were obeying Dorey's orders. There was a time when I began to wonder if you had turned double agent, but I decided you wouldn't have the brains for that kind of a job.'

Bruckman nearly fell out of his chair.

'What the hell are you saying? Me . . . a double agent?'

'Relax, Oscar. You'll bust your truss if you go on like this. I decided you weren't a double agent. This T.S. is dynamite, so Dorey must have made a mistake in giving it to you. Right?'

'I'm not talking to you. Hand it over, Girland!' Bruckman leaned forward, his heavy face flushed, his eyes glittering. 'I know you're a crook, but I hope you won't be that low as to start a third world war! Now, hand it over and I'll take it back to Paris.'

'The trouble with you, Oscar,' Girland said sadly, 'is you have no appeal. Don't give me that stuff about a third world war. Dorey started this. He picked on me, and he couldn't care less what happened to me, so I couldn't care less what happens to him. Just what had he in mind? And, Oscar, don't try any bright lying. I haven't been wasting my time since I've been here. I know all about Mala Reid. Let's have the whole story, then I could give you the T.S., but you're not getting it until I know the story.'

Bruckman's eyes shifted to the gun on the table.

'Oh, Oscar, don't revert to type,' Girland said, watching him. 'The T.S. is somewhere where you won't find it, but if you murder me—as I know you're longing to—sooner or later, Mr. Kosygin will have it. Now, come on, what was this plan Dorey dreamed up in his retarded mind?'

Bruckman hesitated.

'How do I know if I tell you, you'll hand it over?' he demanded.

'Well, of course, you don't know, but I will. Don't laugh right now, but you will have to trust me.'

'One of these days,' Bruckman said furiously, 'I'll fix you! Make no mistake about that! I'll fix you for good!'

'What dialogue,' Girland said, shutting his eyes. 'Boy! Have you missed your vocation! Television would love you.'

Bruckman considered his position. He wondered if he should cable Dorey for further instructions. This situation was something he couldn't handle. Then he remembered what Dorey had told him . . . *make any deal.*

His job was to get this document back to Dorey. It was then up to Dorey to take it from there.

'Okay,' he said. 'This was the setup,' and he told Girland of Dorey's plan to use him as a smoke screen to get Latimer into Prague.

Girland listened, his eyes closed. When Bruckman stopped talking, Girland opened his eyes and smiled at Bruckman.

'So the money is in the wooden angel?'

81

'It's there. I put it there myself.'

'Dorey! What a lovable little midget he's turned out to be,' Girland said. 'Well, I guess he has reason to try to fix me. I'll give him that. Okay, Oscar, now we go to work.' He sat up and swung his legs off the bed. 'Tonight, you will go to Mala's apartment and collect the money. I'll be watching on the sidelines. We will meet at the airport. You will give me the money . . . I will give you the T.S. You will then fly off to Paris and give Dorey my love. But don't get any bright ideas about alerting the police that I will be leaving with thirty thousand dollars. I assure you, if they arrest me, I'll buy myself out of trouble by telling them the contents of the T.S. Does all this sink into the thing you call a brain?'

Bruckman glared at him.

'I couldn't have believed any decent American could act like this,' he said. 'All you think about is money. You are . . .'

'Oh, skip it, Oscar. You'll have me sobbing on your shoulder. What's so wrong about money anyway?' He got up and walked to the door which he opened. 'Shove off.'

Bruckman put his gun into its holster and walked out into the corridor.

'Tonight, around ten-thirty,' Girland said. 'I'll be there, watching. So long for now, Oscar, and watch your blood pressure.' He closed the door as Bruckman walked heavily towards the elevator.

* * *

Smernoff came into the big, sparsely furnished office and closed the door. Malik, dwarfing the desk at which he was sitting, glanced up, pushing aside a pile of decoded cables that had arrived an hour or so ago from Moscow; cables of no interest to him, but which he had to read to keep abreast with G.R.U.'s European activities.

'Well?'

Smernoff pulled up a chair and sat down.

'The situation develops,' he said. 'I have a photograph

that will interest you.' He took from his brief-case a glossy print which he handed to Malik.

Malik looked at the photograph. His expression didn't change, but his green eyes darkened.

'Girland!' he said quietly.

'It was pure luck. I told Zernov to photograph everyone leaving the building, and this fish comes into the net.'

'Girland,' Malik repeated, then sat for some moments, thinking. Finally, he said, 'He could be Worthington's replacement.' He looked at Smernov. 'This surprises me. I thought Girland had fallen out of favour.' He frowned. 'I can't see Girland as Worthington's replacement, can you? Something's wrong here. Girland would have no reason to stay in Prague. The man who will replace Worthington will work here . . . have a job here . . . we know Girland never works.'

'Could be a temporary replacement until the permanent man arrives.'

Malik shook his head.

'Dorey doesn't work like that.' He thought again. 'Girland could be a smoke screen. Could be Dorey wants us to think he is the replacement.'

Smernoff shrugged. It was Malik's job to do the thinking.

'Anything else?' Malik asked, still staring at the photograph.

'The Reid girl went this morning to the apartment of Karel Vlast who was out. I've checked on Vlast. He is suspect,' Smernoff said. 'At one time he was an engraver, now he is a night elevator attendant. Şuk suspects that he fakes passports. He has no proof.'

'And this woman went to see him? She may be trying to get out,' Malik said. 'Why hasn't Suk arrested this man, Vlast?'

'He says he has no proof against him . . . just suspicions.'

'We don't need proof,' Malik said angrily. 'Arrest him and question him. Have his place searched. If he fakes passports, there will be evidence. Do it at once.'

Smernoff got to his feet.

'And Girland?'

'Knowing Girland, he will be at the Alcron.' The corners of Malik's lips turned down. 'He always believes in luxury. Have him watched, but leave him alone for the time being. He could lead us to Worthington. Make sure he doesn't find out he is being watched.'

'And the girl?'

'Leave her alone too. She could also lead us to Worthington. I want her room bugged. When she leaves tonight, send Zernov to her place. If Girland's been there, he will go again. I want a record of their conversation.'

'I'll arrange it,' Smernoff said and left the office.

Malik picked up the photograph and again stared at it. The last time he and Girland had clashed, he had warned Girland when they next met, it would be their last meeting. With slow, savage viciousness, he tore up the photograph.

* * *

For the past hour Mala had discussed Girland's visit with Worthington. They kept asking each other who this man was, who was Harry Moss, was this man one of Dorey's agents, looking for Worthington?

Worthington was nervous. He had hidden in the bathroom while Mala had talked to Girland, fingering his automatic, his body cold with the sweat of fear.

'I just don't know,' he said finally in exasperation. 'We can't go on and on like this. He might be harmless. We mustn't work ourselves up for nothing.' He looked at his watch. 'Isn't it time you went to Vlast?'

Mala nodded.

'All right . . . yes, I'll go.'

Worthington had taken a number of photographs of her for the passport. He gave her the film cartridge.

'He'll want at least three hundred dollars.' He took a fifty dollar bill from his wallet. 'Give him this. Tell him we will pay the rest when he has the passport ready.'

As Mala was leaving the apartment, Karel Vlast was sitting at his window nursing his aching hand. He had been to the hospital that morning. They had given him a shot of something, but it hadn't done much good. He could see by the expression on the doctor's face that his hand was bad. The doctor told him to come back the next day. As he sat at the window, worrying about Worthington's passport, he saw a black Tetra car pull up in the street below. Four men spilled out of the car and walked quickly across the street and entered his apartment block.

Vlast felt his heart contract. He knew these men were from the Security Police. For the past two years he had been expecting just such a visit. He got hurriedly to his feet. He had his preparations ready. He took off the top of his dining table and wedged the oak board under the door handle of his front door. From the top of the cupboard in his tiny hall, he took a hammer and two six-inch nails. Breathing heavily, he hammered the two nails into the floor to act as an additional wedge for the board that now barricaded the front door.

He could hear the tramping feet as the four men climbed the stairs. He reckoned it would take some fifteen minutes to batter down the door. It might, with luck, take them even longer. This was a precaution he had long ago planned to give himself time to destroy any evidence that might incriminate his friends.

He returned to the sitting-room. Opening a cupboard, he took out a large tin box, the lid tightly sealed with tape. He ripped off the tape and tossed the petrol soaked rags the box contained into the fireplace. As the front door bell rang, he lumbered into his bedroom, pulled out the bottom drawer in his chest of drawers, groped into the space and took out a number of passport blanks. The front door bell rang again. He groped into the back of the chest and found Worthington's photographs, his passport and two more photographs of friends he had promised to help.

He heard his front door creak as powerful shoulders thudded against it. He carried the passports, the photographs and several envelopes containing information he needed to complete a faked passport into the sitting-room and dropped them into the fireplace, then as his front door began to come loose at its hinges, he struck a match and set the petrol soaked rags into a violent blaze. The front door began to split down the panels under the violence of the men in the passage. Vlast was quite calm. He picked up the poker and stirred the blazing mass of papers, scattering the ashes, making sure there would be nothing left to betray his friends. Then satisfied, he took from his waistcoat pocket a tiny capsule he had carried around with him for months for such an emergency as this. He slipped the capsule into his mouth and sat down heavily in his favourite dusty armchair.

The door was now half ripped open. He looked across the room at Smernoff whose sweating face was vicious with fury. He waited that extra second until Smernoff was forcing his squat, broad shouldered body through the smashed doorway, then with a murmured prayer, he bit down on the capsule.

* * *

Worthington heard Mala coming up the stairs. He had now come to recognise her step and he got to his feet. For the past hour, he had been in a state of acute anxiety. He had tried to assure himself that Vlast's injury was only trifling, and in a day or so, he would have the passports ready, but at the back of his mind, there was a nagging warning that it was not going to be that easy. Yet in spite of the danger, he was now almost enjoying his stay with Mala. Their close association and now she had agreed to go with him to Geneva, helped to still his fears. He had dreaded the thought of leaving Prague and passing through the Police Control alone. But with Mala, he could face the ordeal. In protecting her, he would forget about himself.

He went to the door when he heard Mala fumbling for her key and opened it. One look at her white, tense face sent a cold chill crawling up his spine.

She came quickly into the room and Worthington shut the door.

'What's happened?' His voice was so husky, he had to clear this throat.

She walked over to a chair and sat down, dropping her bag on the floor.

86.

'He's dead. They were taking him away when I arrived. He's dead.'

Worthington stood petrified. This couldn't be true. He collapsed in a chair opposite hers.

'There must be some mistake . . .' The words came from him in a terrified croak.

'The Security Police were there. There was an ambulance. They were bringing his body out on a stretcher as I passed.' Worthington marvelled at the steadiness of her voice. 'The blanket, covering him, slipped as they put him in the ambulance. I saw him . . . he was dead.'

Worthington put his hands to his face and he shuddered. His hopes for the future, the money he had so painfully and carefully hoarded in Geneva, his plan to escape were wiped out with Vlast's death. There was no chance now, he told himself, of ever getting out of Prague.

Mala watched him. His despair stiffened her morale.

'We have the money,' she said. 'We could still get away.'

Worthington heard, but he knew this was worthless talk. Without a cleverly faked passport, it was impossible to get away. He made the effort and pulled himself together. He must now think of her and not of himself. He must leave her. She might not last long, but she would last longer if he wasn't with her. He thought of the automatic under his arm. The best way would be to walk out of here, find some quiet spot and then shoot himself. He flenched at the idea. Would he find the courage to pull the trigger when the cold barrel was touching his forehead?

'Alec!' Mala's voice had sharpened. 'Are you listening to what I am saying? We have all this money . . . thirty thousand dollars! Surely we can make use of it. We must make use of it! We can buy passports! We can still get away!'

He lifted his head and stared at her, his eyes glazed.

'I know of no one except Vlast and he is dead. There must be someone here who could fake a passport . . . who would accept a large bribe . . . but who?'

Mala got up and began to move around the room. She now realised that she must depend on herself to get them out of this situation. She was aware of a sudden protective feeling for this tall, weak Englishman. He had planned to save her, now she felt compelled to try to save him. She suddenly thought of Jan Braun.

'I know someone who will help us,' she said and came back to her chair. She sat down. 'His name is Jan Braun. His father and my father were close friends. They were executed together. Jan is a farmer. He has a small farm thirty kilometres outside Prague. He could know someone who would get us passports. I'll go and see him.'

Worthington looked hopefully at her.

'Are you sure you can trust him?'

'Of course. His father died with mine . . . of course, I can trust him.'

Watching her, Worthington felt a new hope growing in him. He could see she was no longer frightened. Miraculously, she had become the dominant force of this uneasy partnership.

'He brings his produce to Prague every week,' Mala went on. 'Tomorrow is market day. I'll go to the market and tell him what is happening.'

Worthington wiped his face with his soiled handkerchief.

'No. I'm going to leave you, Mala. This could involve you. I don't want that to happen. No . . . I'll leave you. I'll find a way . . .'

'Oh, be quiet!' she said impatiently. 'Where would you go? Be sensible!' She suddenly smiled at him. 'You tried to help me . . . now, it is my turn.' She got to her feet. 'I'll get supper. It's getting late.'

Worthington remained in his chair while she went into the kitchenette. He thought with bitterness: God! How weak and useless I am!

He had no appetite for the steak she grilled, but he forced himself to eat. Looking at him, seeing how frightened and hopeless he looked, she suddenly reached out and patted his hand.

'It'll work out, Alec,' she said. 'We'll get away.' She got to her feet. 'I must get ready or I'll be late.'

'Yes, of course.' Near to tears, Worthington went behind the screen and lay on the bed.

When Bruckman left Girland, he went immediately to his hotel. In his bedroom, sitting on the bed, a cigarette burning between his thin lips, he put through a call to Paris. There was some delay, then a voice said, 'International Credit.'

'This is Bruckman, speaking from Prague. I had your telegram about those invoices.'

'Yes, Mr. Bruckman. Will you hold a moment, please?'

Bruckman waited. He knew he was being put through to Dorey. It was only in an emergency that he was permitted to call International Credit that would route an agent direct to the C.I.A. This was an emergency. Bruckman felt he had to have confirmation that his deal with Girland would be approved.

'Yes, Mr. Bruckman?' He recognised Dorey's voice.

'Those missing invoices,' Bruckman said. 'Our third party found them. We are arranging a deal. It's cash on delivery. Okay?'

There was a pause, then Dorey said, 'You have the money deposited with you?'

'Yes, but there'll be no change. Still okay?'

'It'll have to be.' Dorey's voice sounded sour. 'I told you . . . you have a free hand,' and the line went dead.

Bruckman grimaced and hung up.

A little after ten o'clock, he left the hotel and took a tram that brought him within easy walking distance to Mala's apartment. He arrived in the street a minute or so before ten-thirty. He saw no sign of Girland, but he knew Girland was concealed in some dark doorway, watching him.

At this moment, Zernov had decided it would be safe to plant the bug Smernoff have given him in Mala's apartment. He was mounting the stairs as Bruckman entered the lobby. Zernov heard him and looked over the banister rail. He could vaguely make out a heavily built man, starting to climb the stairs. Zernov took off his shoes and ran silently up to the fifth floor. He could hear Bruckman's heavy approaching tread. Worthington also heard it. Jumping to his feet, Worthington turned off the light and darted out on to the balcony, carefully closing the french windows after him. He crouched down behind the shrub.

Bruckman reached Mala's front door and rang the bell, watched by Zernov who had gone up the next flight of stairs and was peering at Bruckman through the banister rails.

Bruckman satisfied himself there was no one in the apartment, then he picked the lock and walked in, turning on the light and shutting the door.

Watched by Worthington, Bruckman went immediately to the angel, lifted off the head and reached down into the body. He pulled out the brown paper parcel, replaced the head and moved quickly to the door. He hadn't been in the apartment more than a minute or so. He turned off the light, stepped out on to the dark landing, relocked the door and then using a small flashlight, he started down the stairs.

Zernov watched him. He saw Bruckman was now carrying a brown paper parcel in his left hand. This could be important for Zernov was sure Bruckman hadn't had the parcel when he had entered the apartment. He decided he had to know what the parcel contained. Drawing his gun and leaving his shoes on the stairs, he sneaked silently down to the landing as Bruckman made his way heavily and slowly to the street level, lighting the stairs with the beam of his flashlight.

Zernov groped and found the time switch button that controlled the light on the stairs. He turned the switch on. Light flared up on the stairs. Bruckman spun around, dropping his flashlight, his hand whipping out his automatic. His movements were so swift, Zernov was taken by surprise. Bruckman saw him at the head of the staircase and immediately fired. The bang of the gun crashed through the silent building. Zernov staggered back. Bruckman's bullet had ripped through his sleeve, nicking his forearm, but even as he staggered, he fired three times, and his aim was more deadly than Bruckman's.

Hit in the chest and the left arm, Bruckman fell backwards, rolling and sliding down the stairs to the second

90

landing. The time switch, set only for a minute and working badly, turned off the light.

Cursing, Zernov, his arm burning, blood dripping down his fingers, once again groped for the switch, but couldn't find it. He heard Bruckman get to his feet and start, with stumbling feet, down the stairs.

Realising Bruckman might get away, not knowing how badly he had wounded him, Zernov started down the stairs in pursuit.

Bruckman heard him coming. He turned and fired up the stairs. The bullet whipped past Zernov's face. He crouched down in the darkness and waited, then he heard Bruckman resume his stumbling descent. The big man was moving slowly now.

Shot through the lungs, Bruckman knew this was his finish. He could scarcely breathe and was slowly drowning in his blood, but his toughness kept him moving. He forced his body down the last flight of stairs and he staggered into the lobby. He paused there, still clutching the brown paper parcel under his left arm. He spat blood, then moved slowly and heavily, like a stricken elephant, out into the dimly lit street.

Zernov crept down into the lobby. Bruckman's broad back, outlined against the street lights, made a perfect target. Lifting his gun, Zernov squeezed the trigger.

Bruckman reared back, then fell on his side, the brown paper parcel falling into the gutter.

Nicalok, hearing the shooting, came charging down into the street, gun in hand, from the opposite building.

Girland watched from a nearby doorway. He saw Bruckman fall and the parcel slide from under his arm into the gutter. He had drawn his automatic, but the sudden blare of police sirens warned him it would be too dangerous to attempt to get the parcel.

He ran silently down the street, keeping in the shadows, and ducked down the first narrow lane he came to as the police cars skidded to a halt.

Moving quickly, he headed back to his hotel. That was that, he thought in disgust. Thirty thousand dollars down the drain! Well, he would pack and get out. There was now no point in staying in Prague. Then he thought of the T.S. document. There was now no Bruckman to take it back to Dorey. Why should you care? he asked himself, but he found he was slowing his pace and abruptly he came to a standstill, leaning against a shabby wall while his thoughts were busy. To hell with Dorey! he tried to tell himself. Then he grimaced. He couldn't let a document of that importance fall into Russian hands. You sucker! he said to himself. He thought for some minutes. There was Malik to take into consideration. Girland knew he couldn't hope to leave the country without being searched. Then he remembered Mala Reid. She was one of Dorey's agents. It must be her job to get the papers to Dorey.

Girland decided he would contact her, and slightly cheered, he looked around for a taxi. He was lucky to find one after a patient wait and was driven to the Alhambra night club. As he walked into the shattering noise of swing music and the buzz of voices, a waiter came out of the darkness.

'I'm sorry, sir, we have no free tables.'

Girland took a ten dollar bill from his wallet.

'Squeeze me in somewhere,' he said, allowing the waiter to get a good glimpse of the bill. 'I want some privacy.'

The bill changed hands.

'I have a booth reserved for eleven-thirty, sir. You could have it for half an hour.'

'That's fine,' Girland said and followed the waiter along a narrow corridor to a small booth with a table set for four that looked directly on to the miniature stage.

'Would this do, sir?' the waiter asked.

'Yeah . . . don't run away.' Girland grimaced at the sound coming from the stage. Four under-dressed, unattractive girls were singing. Their shrill, untrained voices magnified by the microphone, beat against his ear drums. He sat down at the table, took a blank card from his wallet and wrote: *Would you join me? I am interested in buying your angel.* He gave the card to the waiter. 'Give this to Miss Mala Reid, and make yourself another ten bucks.'

The waiter gaped at him, read the card and then grinned.

'Yes, sir. Do you want dinner?'

'No . . . I want Miss Reid . . . hurry it up, Comrade.'

When the waiter had gone, Girland sat back in the semidarkness and listened to the noise the four girls were making. Their act finally finished and a few subdued lights came on. It was obviously the interval. He lit a cigarette and continued to wait.

Ten minutes later, the door of the booth pushed open and Mala came in. She was still wearing her blue frock. She had been about to change when the waiter had brought Girland's message. She was very tense and her eyes showed her alarm. When she saw Girland, she started back, half turned to run, then stopped, staring at him.

'Hello, baby,' Girland said, getting to his feet. 'Come on in.' He had to raise his voice to be heard above the noise of the people talking in the restaurant below. 'Remember me? Yes, I see you do. Don't look so scared. I'm always nice to lovely women.'

Mala remained motionless, staring at him, terrified.

'What—what do you want?'

'Sit down,' Girland said. 'Relax. You and I have lots to talk about. Would you like a drink?'

'No . . . what do you want?'

'Sit down.' Girland pulled out a chair. 'You don't have to be scared of me. Come on . . . sit down.'

Very tense, reluctantly, Mala took the chair.

Girland said quietly, 'Now watch carefully . . . this mean anything to you?' He touched the knot of his tie, ran his thumbs down the back of his coat lapels and tapped his right shoulder with his left hand. This was a combination of signals that all Dorey's agents used when they contacted other agents they didn't know.

Mala recognised the signals. She knew then this handsome, very dashing looking American had come from Dorey, but that didn't still her fears.

She nodded.

'Fine,' Girland said. 'Now listen carefully . . . you have a job to do.' He began to tell her about Dorey's plan to use him as a smoke screen, but Mala interrupted him.

'Stop! I don't want to hear! I'm not working for him any more! Don't tell me anything!'

Girland regarded her, his eyes hardening.

'You are Dorey's agent in Prague, aren't you? What are you talking about?'

'I'm not working any more for him!' Mala said desperately. She got to her feet. 'I don't want anything to do with you!'

'You'll have something to do with me,' Girland said. 'Sit down!'

She hesitated, then seeing the expression in his eyes, she obeyed.

'You've reached a point of no return,' Girland said. 'Now listen . . .' Speaking briefly, he told her of Dorey's plan to get Latimer into Prague, how Dorey had made him the smoke screen, and about the thirty thousand dollars. He went on to tell her about Bruckman's part and how he had been shot. 'So the money's gone,' Girland concluded. 'We are now landed with a Top Secret document that must be got back to Dorey. I can't get it out. Malik knows too much about me. It is now up to you . . .' He paused as he saw she was shaking her head.

'He didn't get the money. We found it. It's on the base of the angel,' she said.

'We? Who is we?'

Mala hesitated. There was something about this man that inspired her with confidence. He was so unlike Worthington. She felt, if anyone could help her this man would. She told him about Worthington.

Girland listened, suppressing a groan.

There was a tap on the door. Both stiffened as the door opened. Worthington, wearing his horn spectacles and carrying his suitcase, came into the booth.

chapter five

Malik ripped open the brown paper parcel that had been found by Bruckman's body. He glared at the two folded newspapers, then went through them rapidly to see if there was anything marked, then flung them to the floor.

He looked at Zernov who was nursing a heavily bandaged arm.

'You killed a man for this?'

· Only Smernoff who knew Malik well, realised how close Malik was to explosion point.

Suk who was with Zernov, said, 'He was doing what he thought was right.'

Malik glared at him.

'I wasn't talking to you.' He switched his green eyes to Zernov. 'You killed a man for this?'

'He shot at me,' Zernov said sullenly. 'I had no alternative.'

'This is now an international incident,' Malik said. 'This man is one of Dorey's agents. There will be an inquiry by the American Ambassador. This shooting will make headline news in the Capitalist press. By your stupidity, you have ruined the operation I have arranged. By turning on the light as you did, you have proved yourself a fool and utterly incompetent.'

Zernov's flat, brutal face shone with sweat.

'I—I thought . . .' he stammered but Malik cut him short.

'Thought? How can you think without a brain? Get out!'

Although Malik's face was expressionless, his green eyes

were so malevolent, Zernov recoiled. He hurriedly left the room.

Malik turned and looked at Suk.

'That man must be punished. He is useless to you . . . do you understand?'

'Yes.'

There was a pause, then Malik asked, 'Where is Girland?'

Suk squinted at him.

'Girland? I—I don't know. He is being shadowed. What has he to do with this?'

'Find out where he is! I want to know!'

As Suk made to pick up the telephone, Malik went on, 'Go elsewhere! I need the telephone.'

'Yes.'

Suk hurriedly left the room.

Malik closed his huge hands into fists. Smernoff watched him, feeling it was safer to say nothing. Malik remained still for a long moment, then he said: 'What an operation! You allow Vlast to kill himself! That oaf kills one of Dorey's best men! This woman Reid will be alerted! And then there's Girland . . . can't anything I order be carried out!'

'So what do we do?' Smernoff said. He found Malik's tantrums boring.

Malik stared at him.

'We pick up the girl and Girland. We'll make them talk. I am now handling this myself. I can't trust any of these fools!'

'Suppose we wait for Suk's report?' Smernoff said, lighting a cigarette. 'The girl is at the nightclub now. Her act comes on in fifty minutes. We have time. We can pick her up when she leaves.'

Malik contained himself with an effort.

'Yes . . . give me a cigarette.'

'Why don't you buy your own cigarettes?' Smernoff grumbled and handed over a pack of Benson & Hedges.

'These are capitalist cigarettes,' Malik said.

Smernoff grinned.

'I like them. If you don't want to smoke that kind of cigarette, why should I care?'

Malik lit the cigarette and tossed the pack back to Smernoff.

'Why newspapers in a parcel?' he said, thinking aloud. 'Bruckman broke into the woman's apartment. Let us imagine he was looking for something of value and this woman planted this parcel.' He looked at the newspapers on the floor. 'There might be a hidden message there. They must be examined.'

Suk came into the room, white faced, his forehead moist.

'They have lost him,' he said, his voice despairing. 'I had three men covering him . . . yet, they have lost him!'

Malik made a savage movement with his hand.

'This will be reported, Comrade Suk. Girland is not to leave the country. I hold you personally responsible. I want this man!' Turning to Smernoff, he said, 'We will now pick up the girl. She could tell us where Worthington is hiding. I want him too.' He glared at Suk. 'Have her apartment searched!'

He left the room, followed by Smernoff.

Suk mopped his face, then picked up the telephone receiver. He began to give instructions to every frontier post, the airport and to the guards at the railway station.

'This man must be detained,' he kept saying. 'There must be no mistake.'

* * *

Worthington was telling his story. He sat, huddled down in the chair, facing Mala and Girland. His eyes were wide with alarm.

Hearing the shooting, he explained, he realised that very soon the police would arrive and search the apartment.

'I packed some things for you,' he said, looking at Mala. 'We can't go back. They will be looking for you now. They could come here.'

Girland was examining this tall, weak looking Englishman. He asked himself what the hell he was getting into by being involved with a man like this.

'How about the money?' he asked, watching Worthington closely.

Worthington stiffened, then looked quickly at Mala.

'I've told him,' she said.

Worthington flinched. The money was terribly important to him. How could she have told a complete stranger that they had so much money?

'I don't understand . . . I . . .'

'We'll go into details later,' Girland said crisply. 'What's happened to the money?'

Worthington hesitated and looked for guidance from Mala. Just how much, he wondered, had she told this man?

'He knows about the money,' Mala said impatiently.

Again Worthington hesitated, then said sullenly, 'I have it in my suitcase.'

Girland drew in a long, slow breath.

'That's something . . . now, let's get out of here. You know the district. Where do we go?'

Mala hesitated.

'If we had a car . . . we could go to a friend of mine, Jan Braun. He has a farm.'

'What's so difficult about a car? We'll borrow one. Okay, let's go to your friend. Come on . . . is there a back way out?'

'Yes . . .' Mala was still hesitating.

'Snap it up, baby. The fuse is burning.'

'But I just can't walk out . . .'

Girland caught hold of her arm.

'Let's go!'

Worthington, listening to all this, looking helplessly first at Girland and then at Mala, said, 'He's right. They could come here, looking for you.'

'Today's understatement,' Girland said and bustled Mala out into the passage. 'Lift your pretty feet. Where do we go?'

Galvanised by the hard urgency in his voice, she pulled away from him and ran down the passage to a door. She opened it and stepped out into a dark yard that opened out on to a small parking lot where a number of cars, owned by tourists, stood in a line.

Girland, followed by Worthington, carrying his suitcase, joined her. Girland looked at the line of cars.

'Wait here,' he said and moved quickly to the cars. He checked five of them before he found a Mercedes with the key in the ignition lock. He slid into the driving seat and turned on the parking lights, then he waved to Mala and Worthington to join him. They came across the parking lot at a run. Worthington got into the back seat and Mala scrambled in beside Girland who let in the clutch and drove out of the parking lot.

As he drove down the main street, he saw two police cars pull up outside the entrance to the arcade leading to the night club.

'Nicely timed,' he said and smiled at Mala. 'Now, where do we go?'

Mala directed him out of the City. She kept looking at him as he drove at a steady speed, taking no risks. His calm expression, the sardonic look in his eyes and his smile of relaxation gave her tremendous confidence.

As they crossed the Hiávkûv Bridge, Worthington said, 'We can't hope to get away. They'll trace the car. We . . .'

'Relax,' Girland said. 'The show isn't over for another eighty minutes. This is a tourist's car. It won't be missed until the show is over, then the owner will have to report to the police. Imagine the flap he'll be in, trying to make himself understood. We have at least two hours' start.' He turned to Mala. She was really quite a doll, he thought. He began to warm to her. 'Tell me about Jan Braun.'

Steadying her voice, Mala told him about Braun.

'His farm is only thirty kilometres from here. He'll help us . . . I am sure he will.'

'That's comforting. We need help, baby. We need a lot of help.' They were climbing a steep hill out of the city. Girland went on, 'So you got tired of Dorey?' He was now speaking to Worthington. 'I don't blame you. I got tired of him months ago.'

Reacting to the understanding note in Girland's voice, Worthington leaned forward.

'It was when I heard that Malik had arrived,' he said. 'I knew . . .'

'Malik?' Girland's voice shot up. 'Did you say Malik?'

'Yes.'

'Is he in Prague?'

'Yes . . . he is hunting for me.'

'Phew!' Girland grimaced. Watching him, Mala felt a stab of fear. For a brief moment, Girland looked startled and less confident. He went on, 'Malik and I are old pals. We love each other the way a mongoose loves a snake. Are you sure Malik is in Prague?'

'Yes, I am sure.'

Girland slightly increased the speed of the car while he thought. He now realised the three of them were in deadly danger. He knew Malik. Where Malik was, Smernoff was, and Smernoff was the Soviet's top hunter of men. His long silence, while he thought, terrified both Mala and Worthington.

'Tell me about Braun,' Girland said finally. 'Have you been seen with him? I know Malik. He will check on everyone who is in your circle. If he finds out you know a farmer he will check him right away.'

'I haven't seen Jan now for more than a year,' Mala told him. 'I've never mentioned him to any of my friends. I am sure he will help us because my father helped his father.'

'Have you been to his farm?'

'Once, about three years ago.'

'What sort of place is it?'

'It's run down and lonely . . . really lonely.'

'Is he on his own?'

'He lives with his wife . . . Blanca.'

'Can you trust her?'

'Oh, yes. She is a wonderful woman.'

'He has the usual outhouses?'

'There are two big barns.'

Girland thought, then shrugged.

'Okay, we'll have to take a chance. I don't see what else we can do. We might still need this car for a quick getaway. We could hide it in one of the barns.' He increased speed.

Worthington listening to all this, resented and feared Girland. This man was doing what he knew he should be doing. Worthington was also worried about the money in his suitcase. There was something about Girland that warned him Girland would take the money if he had the chance, and yet Worthington realised bitterly that if anyone could save him, it would be Girland.

Girland was sensitive to a hostile atmosphere. He had already realised that Worthington could become a nuisance. He also realised that this weak, tall man was desperately in love with Mala. This also might complicate the situation. He began to tell Worthington about Dorey's plan to use him as a smoke screen, about Harry Moss, the money and why he had come to Prague.

'Dorey was too smart. He planted on me a T.S. document by mistake,' Girland concluded. 'Now I'm landed with it. If I don't get it back to him, he's through. I happen to have a soft spot for the old goat. He's the salt in my stew.' He laughed. 'Life would be damn dull without him, so I'm going to get it back to him, but the operation will be tricky.'

'Couldn't you give it to the Ambassador?' Mala asked. 'He would get it back to Mr. Dorey.'

'If I gave it to the Ambassador, he would read it. He would see that it was Dorey's personal copy and he would want to know why it was in Prague. No, if I am to save Dorey's hide, I have to get it back to him myself.'

'You have it on you?' Worthington asked, stiff with resentment.

Girland looked briefly at the thin, weak face he could see in the driving mirror.

'I have it. I was going to swap it with Bruckman for the money. It would have been safe with him . . . he was Dorey's man, but now Bruckman is dead, so it falls into my lap.'

There was a pause, then Worthington said, 'This money belongs to me. Mala and I need it to get out of the country. You're not having it. That must be understood.'

Here it comes, Girland thought, then said quietly, 'Nothing should be understood until you get out. Just how do you plan to get out?'

'That is my business!' Worthington said. 'I'm telling you this money is for Mala and me, and you're not having it!'

Girland slowed the car, then brought it to a standstill. As he swung around in his seat, he found himself confronted by Worthington's automatic. Worthington, white faced, his eyes wild, threatened Girland with the gun.

'Give me that document!' Worthington said, his voice shrill and out of control. 'We don't want you with us! Give it to me!'

Girland stared at him, then swinging around, he shoved his foot down on the accelerator.

'Drop dead,' he said as the car took off and began to roar down the long, dark road.

'Stop or I'll . . . I'll . . .' Worthington began helplessly as the car flew down the road at over 120 kilometres an hour.

'Go ahead and shoot,' Girland said calmly. 'It'll be a lovely smash.'

Listening to all this, Mala lost patience.

'Stop it, Alec! Can't you see he is the only one who can save us! Stop behaving so stupidly!'

Worthington wilted. The cold contempt in her voice told him as nothing else could just how useless she thought him.

He returned his gun to its holster and huddled down in his seat.

Girland said, 'Relax, pal. We all get worked up from time to time. There'll be lots of time to arrange who gets what and who gets who.'

'You're not having the money!' Worthington said weakly. 'You may . . .'

'I told you to stop it!' Mala cried, swinging around in her seat and waving her hands at Worthington who subsided into sullen silence.

The car sped on along the narrow, deserted road. The moon lit the distant hills and the forests on either side of the road. They drove for some twenty minutes, then Mala said, 'It is quite close now.'

Girland slowed the car.

'Just here. There's a turning to the left,' Mala said, sitting forward.

Girland brought the car to a stop as he swung left into a narrow lane.

'Go to the farm,' he said. 'Tell your friend you have company. We must be sure of a welcome. If he doesn't want us, we'll have to think where else to go.'

'I'm sure it's all right to drive up. I know he will want to help us,' Mala said.

Girland smiled at her.

'I'm not, and I'm in charge of the operation. Go on, baby, walk.'

Mala got out of the car, hesitated, then started up the lane.

Worthington said angrily, 'You can't order her about like that! Who do you think you are?'

Girland turned, his eyes bleak.

'I'm getting bored with you. You haven't a hope in hell of getting this girl nor yourself out of the country. If anyone can do it, I can, so shut up!'

Worthington made a move to draw his gun. His reflexes were so slow that Girland had his own gun in his hand before Worthington could touch his gun butt.

'Get out of the car!' Girland said. 'Quick . . . before I knock you off!'

Flinching from the threat of the gun, Worthington stumbled out of the car. Girland joined him in the narrow lane, keeping him covered.

'I've had more than enough from you,' he said. 'Turn around and drop your gun!'

Worthington hurriedly obeyed. The gun dropped on to the grass verge.

'Walk forward!'

As Worthington moved a few steps, Girland picked up his gun. He unloaded it and dropped the cartridges into his pocket.

103

'Here,' he said, and as Worthington turned, Girland tossed the gun to him. 'It's safer for both of us unloaded.'

Worthington put the gun back into its holster. His face was pale and his eyes showed his humiliation.

'Now behave,' Girland went on. 'I'm handling this operation. You're just part of the scenery . . . get it?'

Worthington muttered something and turned away.

In silence the two men waited by the Mercedes for Mala to return.

* * *

Suk could scarcely conceal his satisfaction that so important a man as Malik had let Mala Reid slip through his fingers.

He sat by the desk watching Malik who was poring over a large scale map of the district. Malik's eyebrows were drawn down in an ominous frown. It was impossible, he kept assuring himself, that this woman could get out of the country. When they did catch her, he would make her sorry. This was something he would attend to personally.

There came a tap on the door and Smernoff came in.

'Girland's with her,' he announced as he closed the door. 'There is a second man . . . from the description I have it must be Worthington.'

Malik sat back.

'Girland . . . are you sure?'

'A waiter at the night club took a man to a private booth. From his description, there is no doubt that it is Girland. He sent Reid a card saying he was interested in buying her angel. Some minutes later, a tall Englishman joined them. The waiter saw them all leave by the back way which leads to a car park. A Mercedes car is missing.' Smernoff rattled off his report, his flat, black eyes watching Malik's reaction. 'There is a wooden angel in Reid's apartment.'

'You have the number of the Mercedes?'

'I have it here.' Smernoff put a slip of paper on the desk.

Malik gestured to Suk.

104

'Trace this car!'

Taking the slip of paper, Suk rushed out of the room.

There was a pause, then Malik said, 'Have you searched her apartment?'

'Of course.' Smernoff pulled up a chair and sat astride it, resting his thick arms on the chair's back. 'Worthington has been hiding there. We found his finger prints and some of his clothes. Bruckman's prints are on this wooden angel. The head comes off and there is a hollow space in the body. Something was obviously hidden there . . . probably, the brown paper parcel.'

Malik thought for a long moment, then he said, 'They have a fast car. They will have left the city. It is possible they will make for the frontier. The German border is the nearest, but they could make for the Austrian border . . . the crossing there is much easier.'

Smernoff shrugged.

'I am having Reid's dossier checked. It is unlikely they will try to cross the frontier immediately. It's my guess they will go into hiding, and when they think the search has slackened, then they will make their attempt. We must find their hiding place. I'll see what her dossier has to tell us.'

Malik nodded, and as Smernoff moved to the door, Malik said, 'We have to find them. I don't have to tell you what it will mean if they escape.'

Smernoff grinned evilly.

'What makes you think they can escape?'

He went out, shutting the door.

Ten minutes later as Malik was again examining the map, Suk came in.

'The car was seen crossing Hiávkûv Bridge,' he reported. 'There is no further news of it. There were three people in the car: a man driving, a woman by his side and another man at the back.'

Malik looked up, his eyes menacing.

'Your job, Comrade, is to see they don't cross the frontier. I don't care how many men you use! These three must not cross the frontier!'

'I am arranging that now,' Suk said. 'They won't get across.'

Malik dismissed him with an impatient wave of his hand. When Suk had gone, Malik lit a cigarette and stared into space. He was furious with himself. He should have arrested the girl when Smernoff had warned him that Cain was interested in her. He had played it too smart. Savagely, he cursed Girland. He could imagine how Kovski, his boss, would react. The two men hated each other. Up to now, Malik had always been in an unassailable position. He had never made a mistake, but he knew he had made one now and Kovski would take advantage of it.

He was still sitting at the desk an hour later when Smernoff came into the room.

'We have a possible clue,' Smernoff said and laid a snapshot on the desk. 'This was found in a photograph album we took from Reid's apartment.'

Malik studied the photograph. It showed Mala and a young, heavily built man, standing side by side. The man was wearing jeans, a check shirt and mud caked boots. Behind them was a low built farm house. To their right were two big barns.

Malik looked up.

'So?'

'A lonely farm would be an ideal hiding place. It is worth checking.' Smernoff said. 'During the revolution, Reid's father and a farmer named Braun were executed as traitors. His son, Jan Braun, is also a farmer.'

Malik kicked away his chair and jumped to his feet.

'You know where the farm is?'

'Thirty kilometres from here.'

'Get men!'

'I have three police cars waiting. There are twelve men with automatic weapons ready to go.'

'If Girland is with them, we need three times as many men,' Malik said. 'Arrange it!'

'If you say so,' Smernoff said, shrugging and reached for the telephone.

* * *

106

There was no comfort in the big, shabby room with its oak beams, its stone floors and rough deal furniture. The big open fireplace that dominated the room was smoke blackened and a large pile of white ash from previous fires still filled the grate.

Looking around, Girland thought it would be an ice box in the winter. He, Mala and Worthington were on upright chairs facing Jan Braun and his wife who were sitting on a long deal bench, their backs to the fireplace.

Jan Braun was a heavily built man in his early thirties. His round, fleshly face, his firm mouth and steady slate grey eyes inspired confidence.

Blanca, his wife, was some five years younger: a blonde girl with a plain, serious face, slimly built, and who radiated a serene calmness that pleased Girland. He was sure she could be relied on in any emergency.

The Brauns were wearing well-worn jeans and black wind-cheaters. They had been in bed when Mala had hammered on the farm house door. She had told them that she and two friends were in trouble, would they help? They hadn't hesitated. While Mala had run back down the lane, they had scrambled into their clothes. Jan had opened the doors of one of the barns and Girland had driven the Mercedes under cover.

Girland was now doing the talking.

'You don't want to know too much about this operation,' he was saying. 'The less you know, the safer for you two and for us. We must get across the frontier. This is a top priority: a treble must with all kinds of international explosions if we don't. So I repeat: we must get across the frontier. We have a G.R.U. agent—the best there is—after us. Money is no object. We have plenty of that, and we will buy our way out if it can be arranged.'

Jan studied Girland, then shook his head.

'It won't be money that will get you across the frontier,' he said quietly. 'It will be luck. None of you has a hope of passing through the police control with a false passport. That is a pipe dream. The frontier restrictions between here and Austria have been eased recently, but they still have the organisation to make a shut-down at a moment's

107

notice. If your G.R.U. agent thinks you are important enough, he can call out troops, and the whole frontier will be completely sealed.' He paused and then went on, 'But there is a place where a crossing is possible. It is some hundred and thirty kilometres from here. It will mean walking. The going will be rough. A four day journey, averaging thirty kilometres a day.'

Girland grimaced. He couldn't imagine Mala walking that distance.

'Can't we use a car?'

'They will be watching the roads. No, it would be too risky. The only safe way is to walk, and to keep off the roads.'

Quick to realise how useful Jan would be to them, Girland said, 'Suppose you two come with us. We could finance you. Why not?'

Jan and Blanca exchanged glances.

'We couldn't do that,' Jan said, but there was doubt in his voice.

'Do you want to live here for ever? What's your future in this country? Once out, you can make a fresh start.' Girland looked around the shabby room. 'You've got nothing here have you . . . you're getting nowhere, are you? Here's my proposal: we have thirty thousand dollars. There are five of us. I suggest we split the money five ways. You two will get twelve thousand. With that kind of money, you could make a fresh start in Austria . . . Germany . . . France . . . anywhere you like.'

Worthington clutched hold of his suitcase.

'You have no right to make such an offer!' he exclaimed wildly. 'This money doesn't belong to you . . . it belongs to Mala and me!'

The four looked at him, then Mala said quietly, 'It doesn't belong to us, Alec. Please don't be stupid.'

'You're always telling me that I'm stupid!' Worthington cried hysterically. 'Can't you see, I'm trying to protect your interests? This money . . .'

'Alec! Will you please stop this!' Mala said. She got to her feet and crossed to Worthington. 'Give me the suitcase.'

Worthington looked hopelessly at her and then gave her the suitcase.

'Take it,' he said, his voice shaking with emotion. 'You are giving away your future. You think I am stupid, but it is you who don't realise what you are doing.'

'Yes, I do . . . we are buying our freedom,' Mala said and pointing to the suitcase, she went on to Girland, 'The money's there. You deal with it.'

Girland nodded. To Jan he said, 'Twelve thousand dollars . . . it's yours if you take us across the frontier. It's up to you if you return here or not.'

Jan hesitated, then got to his feet.

'We must discuss this,' he said. 'Excuse us,' and putting his hand on Blanca's arm, he led her from the room.

Girland opened the suitcase and found the packet of money.

'These two know the country,' he said to Mala. 'They speak the language and they know how we can get out. We can't do without them . . . that's why I'm offering them the money.'

Mala nodded.

'Yes, of course . . . I understand.'

'You can afford to give the money away,' Worthington said bitterly. 'It's easy for you. You can blackmail Dorey for three times the amount you are giving away.'

Girland regarded him with unconcealed impatience.

'If you feel so strongly about it, you can get the hell out of here. Your share is on the table . . . six thousand dollars. You don't have to come with us. Take your share and go back to Prague.'

Worthington glowered at him.

'You know I can't do that!'

'Why should I care what you do? You have your share . . . do what you like, but if you come with us, you will pull your weight and you'll stop being a pest!'

Worthington turned to Mala.

'This man is a crook. Can't you see that? He has already taken the money that belongs to you. He . . .'

'The money doesn't belong to me!' Mala said, her voice exasperated. 'Will you stop talking this nonsense!'

109

Worthington looked helplessly at her, then shrugged in despair.

'Very well . . . then I will say nothing.'

While this was going on, Girland was looking around the room, bored with Worthington. He saw on the overmantel a framed photograph. He glanced at it, then away, then stiffening, he got to his feet and walked over to the photograph to examine it closely. It was of Mala and Jan with the farm building and the farm house in the background. He turned quickly.

'This photograph . . . have you a copy of it?'

Mala looked at the photograph and realised at once what he was thinking. She turned white.

'Yes . . . it's in an album at my apartment.'

Girland lifted his hands.

'Well, that's it then.' He went to the door. 'Hey, you two! Come back here!'

Jan and Blanca came from the bedroom. As they entered the living-room, Jan said, 'We have decided. We will come with you.'

Girland smiled crookedly.

'You now have no choice.' He pointed to the photograph. 'Mala has this in her apartment. They will find it. It won't take them long to identify the farm. They could be here in a couple of hours. We have to get moving. Here, take your share.' He gave Jan a packet of the dollar bills. 'Come on, we must get moving.'

Jan stared at the money, then hurriedly put it in his hippocket.

'Blanca . . .' He waved to Mala. 'She can't travel in those clothes. Find her something. I'll get things together,' and he hurried out of the room.

Putting her arm around Mala's shoulders, Blanca said, 'He's right. Come with me. I'll see what I can find for you.' The two girls went into the bedroom.

Girland and Worthington eyed each other. Worthington started to say something, but the bored look in Girland's eyes stopped him. Girland lit another cigarette and then waved to the money on the table.

'Take your share, and listen, while we have a moment

110

together. If I have any further trouble with you, you won't know what's hit you. This is tricky enough without you trying to gum up the works.'

Worthington flushed. With an unsteady hand he took his share of the money and put it in his pocket.

Girland grinned at him.

'Relax. Don't look so tragic. If we're going to save our skins, we've all got to work together.'

Worthington walked over to the window and stared out into the dark night. Girland eyed him, then shrugged. After a ten-minute wait, Jan came back with three bulging rucksacks.

'I've collected all the food we have . . . there's some canned stuff, candles, soap, matches and a blanket each . . . it'll have to do,' he said, dropping the rucksacks on the floor. 'We have a long hike.'

Blanca and Mala came into the room. Mala was wearing a pair of faded jeans, a sweater and stout walking shoes. Girland thought the shabby clothes set off her figure very well.

'What's the first move?' Girland asked as he gave Mala her share of the money.

'I have a hut in the hills,' Jan said. 'We'll go there first. It is ten kilometres from here. Once there, we'll be safe to make plans. I have maps and can show you the route we will have to take.' He put two big paper bags on the table. 'This is pepper. They will have tracker dogs with them. Sooner or later, I knew we would have to go on the run and I've been hoarding pepper for months. We'll walk in single file. I go first.' He looked at Girland. 'You will be last. You take the pepper. Scatter it carefully behind you. It should last at least two kilometres . . . that will be enough. Now, let's go.'

Five minutes later, the five of them started across the rough grass in single file. Girland had made a tiny hole in one of the paper bags and was allowing the pepper to fall behind him. Soon, away from the farm, they began to climb through a forest of firs. The tree studded, rocky slope leading up to the hill was hard going. Jan set the pace, and Mala had trouble in keeping up. Blanca, used to

111

this kind of climbing, swung along easily. Every now and then Girland had to come forward to help Mala.

Worthington climbed sullenly behind Jan without looking back. He carried his suitcase awkwardly. He was dismayed and furious that Girland should have split the money the way he had. Twelve thousand dollars to these two small time farmers! It was ridiculous! They would have been happy with a third of such a sum, he kept thinking.

They branched off on to a narrow path, coming out of the forest, and Jan began to move even faster. After climbing for ten minutes or so, Mala wailed, 'I must stop . . . I can't go on!'

The party paused. Jan looked impatiently at her.

'We still have some way to go.'

'Look!' Girland said and pointed down the hill.

Away in the distance they could see the narrow lane, like a white ribbon in the moonlight, that led to the farm house. Coming up the lane were cars, looking like toys from that distance . . . ten of them, strung out and moving fast.

'Here they come!' Girland said and yanked Mala to her feet. 'Come on, baby.'

Galvanised by the tone of his voice, Mala started after the others. Stumbling, sweating and panting, the small party struggled upwards until they reached a plateau where they had an uninterrupted view of the farm far below. They could see lights showing at every window and ant-like figures moving around the farm and the outbuildings.

'The pepper's finished,' Girland said.

'It'll be enough,' Jan returned. 'This next bit is rough. Let's take it easy . . . it leads to the hut.'

He began to force his way through the undergrowth, off the path, and the others followed. If Girland hadn't constantly helped Mala, she would never have made the climb. Worthington, sulking and still furious, didn't look back although he knew Mala was in difficulties. Finally, after an exhausting half hour's climb they came to a log cabin, set on a plateau, overhung with trees. It was practically invisible until they came right on it.

'This is it,' Jan said and unlocked the cabin door. 'It's not much, but it will be safe.'

Blanca took a torch from her rucksack and lit the way in. The big room was damp and smelt musty. There was a table, a few stools and four bunks on the walls.

While Jan was lighting the candles, Mala, scarcely able to drag one foot after the other, headed for one of the bunks.

'Don't lie in that!' Blanca said sharply. 'There could be a snake in there!'

Mala lost her fatigue so quickly as she sprang back that Girland burst out laughing.

'Okay, baby, I'll look,' he said and taking the torch, he examined the bunk, turning the mattress cautiously. 'Not a snake . . . a spider or two, but no snakes.'

Mala shuddered and sat on a stool. Worthington stood by the door, still holding his suitcase, his thin face tight with fatigue, his eyes hostile and suspicious.

Girland unpacked the rucksacks and got the blankets while Jan started a fire in the small grate. Blanca joined Girland and found coffee, a tin of powdered milk, mugs and a saucepan.

Ten minutes later, they were all sitting around the table, sipping strong, scalding coffee and trying to relax.

By now the fire had caught hold and the dry logs were spitting and blazing, sending a cheerful glow around the dimly lit room. Girland passed his pack of Pall Mall around the table. Mala took one gratefully. Both Jan and Blanca shook their heads. Worthington hesitated, then shoved the pack back to Girland. He lit his own cigarette. The warmth and the coffee acted as an antidote to their aching muscles.

Jan took a map from his pocket and spread it on the table.

'This is the way we have to go,' he said. 'If we could go by road and in a car, it would be half a day's journey, but the way we have to go, will be tough.'

He traced the journey with a thick finger. To Mala, watching, it seemed his finger went on for ever across the

113

map before it finally stopped at the Czech-Austrian frontier.

'We cross here, if we have any luck,' Jan went on. He paused and tilted back his chair. 'I'll tell you what the frontier is like. First, you have the watch towers, equipped with men, a machine gun, signal rockets, searchlights and a radio telephone. These men have an uninterrupted view as all trees, shrubs and other obstructions have been cleared for seventy metres. The ground approaching the towers has been made into a seed bed and is raked every day so that footprints can clearly be seen. Beyond this seed bed is a barbed wire fence, wired with alarm signals. Then there is a strip of ground sown with anti-personnel mines. Then there is a second fence which is electrified. All this sounds like an impossible barrier . . . it is, but there is one place where we can get through . . . by using an air-shaft in a disused copper mine. Not so long ago, I took a friend through and he got into Austria, but there was no alert out for him as there is for us. This is going to be a very dangerous, tricky operation, but I think . . . given a lot of luck . . . it is possible.'

Girland studied the map. Finally, he looked at Jan.

'When do we start?'

'We should stay here for at least four days,' Jan said. 'By now the whole frontier will have been alerted. I know the Czech troops . . . most of them are boys. For four days, they will be on the alert, then they will get bored and that will be the time to make the crossing.'

'Is it safe to remain here for four days?'

Jan lifted his shoulders.

'I think so. We are well concealed here. My neighbours don't know I have this cabin. I built it two years ago, knowing that sooner or later, we would have to get out. Yes, I think we can stay here safely.'

'Okay,' Girland said. 'Let's get organised. We three men should keep watch. Four hours each. I'll take the first watch.'

'Yes,' Jan said, nodding. 'I'll relieve you. Then our friend here can relieve me.'

114

Worthington nodded sullenly and moving away, began to prepare himself for bed.

Jan and Girland exchanged glances. Girland grimaced, then as Jan began to feed more logs onto the fire, he went out into the darkness to begin his watch.

* * *

Smernoff walked over to where Malik was waiting by one of the police cars.

'They've laid a pepper trail,' he said in a cold, flat voice. 'The dogs can't pick up the scent. They can't have gone far, but we have no idea in which direction they have gone.'

Malik's green eyes glittered. He wasn't interested in excuses.

'This is your job,' he said, a rasp in his voice. 'They must not cross the frontier! You can have as many men as you need. They will walk. They won't use the roads. I don't have to tell you this.' He regarded Smernoff, his expression cold and aloof. 'Find these people. I am returning to the Ministry.' He got into the police car and told the driver to take him back to Prague.

Smernoff watched the car drive away. He grinned. For eight years, he had hunted men and women, and he had yet failed to find them. He knew Malik was worried. This amused him. Malik was always thinking of his reputation. He worried that one day, Kovski, who hated him, would ruin him. Malik minded about being ruined. Smernoff was too tough and indifferent to worry about such mundane things. His job was to hunt people. If he failed, then he didn't deserve to hold his job. It was as simple as that.

He walked over to where Suk was waiting.

'At dawn there must be at least three helicopters combing the hills. See to it! I want now to talk to Captain Kuhlan.'

Kuhlan, a young, ardent Communist, delighted to have orders from such a man as Smernoff, came hurrying up.

'Come with me,' Smernoff said and walked to the farm house. He spread out a large scale map of the district on the table. He produced a compass and inserting the needle end into the spot on the map that showed the farm house, he drew a circle. Suk had joined them and was standing a little behind Smernoff, listening and watching. 'We have two alternatives to consider,' Smernoff said, sitting back and looking at the young Captain. 'They will either make immediately for the frontier or they will hide up somewhere and wait until they imagine the search for them has died down. It is my opinion, they will wait. Somewhere within this circle they will hide. Tomorrow there will be aircraft searching this area. Your job is to move enough men so this circle is encircled. In this way, they will be trapped.' He pushed the map across the table. 'Study the ground, then arrange for as many men as you need to make a tight circle ... I mean tight. Do you understand?'

'Yes, Comrade Smernoff,' Kuhlan said and began to study the map.

Smernoff watched him, pleased with his obvious eagerness. This young blond man was like a tracker dog hunting for a scent as he bent over the map.

Suk said, 'It is only a matter of time.' His voice rang with a false confidence. 'They can't possibly get across the frontier.'

Smernoff ignored him. He continued to watch Kuhlan. After five minutes of careful study, Kuhlan straightened.

'I'll arrange the operation,' he said briskly. 'I know the district well. I know just how many men will be needed. By eight o'clock tomorrow morning, they will be in position.'

Smernoff showed his teeth in a menacing smile.

'They must be in a position by daybreak . . . by six o'clock at the latest.'

'Very well, Comrade Smernoff,' Kuhlan said and he hurriedly left the room.

chapter six

Worthington pulled his worn jacket closer around him and shivered. He was sitting on a flat stone, his back against a rock, looking down into the mist covered valley far below. He had been sitting there since four o'clock and it was nearly half-past six. It had been a damp, cold watch, and he longed for the sun to come up and warm his aching bones. Resentfully, he thought it was typical of Girland to have given him the dawn watch. How he disliked this tall, handsome, cocky man! He knew Girland was without nerves, and he knew women would automatically react to him. He had seen the way Mala had looked at him. She seemed to think he was some kind of god.

He took his depleted pack of cigarettes from his pocket. He had only five left. He hesitated, then unable to resist the urge, he lit one.

He glanced over his shoulder at the dark cabin. There was no movement. They were all sleeping. He stared up at the lightening sky, across the tree tops and once again down into the mist covered valley. He felt a tug of fear at his heart. They would send troops. They would search every inch of the hills. Sooner or later, they would find them.

Worthington flinched at the thought of what would happen to him. His hand touched the butt of his gun, snug in its holster, then he remembered Girland had taken away the bullets. He couldn't even shoot himself, if the soldiers surrounded them.

He sucked in smoke and slowly exhaled. He shifted on the cold rock, trying to make himself comfortable, then he stiffened as he heard a droning sound some distance away.

Outlined against the cloudless sky, he saw a helicopter, flying above the tree tops, down in the valley. He started to his feet, his heart thumping. More sound filled the sky and looking to his left, he saw yet another helicopter.

, He ran towards the cabin as the door swung open and Girland, followed by Jan, appeared.

'Get under cover!' Girland snapped. 'Quick!'

Worthington bolted into the cabin.

Girland and Jan stood under a tree, close to the cabin. They spotted one of the helicopters that was moving directly towards them.

'They're pulling out all the stops,' Girland said.

'They won't see us,' Jan returned quietly. 'The trees cover the cabin. We'll have to stay under cover while the sweep is on. They're likely to spot any movement.'

The sound of the helicopter's engine grew louder. Both men remained motionless, leaning against the trunk of the tree. The helicopter passed directly overhead, flying high and then the sound of its engine began to die away.

They looked at each other.

'They certainly think you're important,' Jan said. 'Let's have some coffee.'

Keeping under the trees, they made their way back to the cabin. The two girls were out of their bunks and looking tense. Worthington stood by the fire, holding cold, shaking hands towards the blaze.

'They won't spot us,' Jan said soothingly. 'Coffee ready?'

'In a minute,' Blanca said. She was very calm, but Mala was frightened. She crossed to Girland.

'Do you think we'll get away?' she asked in a low, unsteady voice.

Girland patted her arm.

'Sure. We will now have to move at night and hide up during the day . . . that's all there is to it.' He looked into her blue eyes. 'You have nothing to be scared about so long as I'm with you.'

She hesitated, then smiled.

'I know . . . you really think we will get out?'

'Sure. It'll be tricky but it can be done.' He resisted the

118

temptation to put his arm around her, seeing Worthington was watching them.

She examined his hard, confident face, then she joined Blanca who was preparing the breakfast.

Catching Worthington's smouldering glare, Girland winked at him before going to the cabin door where Jan was staring through the branches of the trees up at the sky.

'There are three helicopters now,' Jan said.

'We'll have to move at night. If they are staging an operation this size, they will also have a lot of ground troops.'

Jan thought, then he said quietly, 'They can't know which direction we took. They'll make a big circle around the farm and then close in.' He was looking worried.

Both men stiffened as they heard the approaching beat of the helicopter engines. This time the helicopter was flying at tree-top level. They caught a glimpse of it through the trees. It was circling a patch of forest some fifty kilometres from them.

'We'd better put the fire out,' Girland said. 'It's not giving off much smoke but as they're flying this low, they could spot it.'

They moved back into the living-room of the cabin. The girls had heated two tins of sausages and the coffee was made. Jan damped down the fire, spreading the logs before joining the others at the table. The atmosphere was tense. They could hear the helicopter coming closer.

Suddenly it swooshed by the cabin, sending a violent gust of wind that ruffled Mala's hair and made her stifle a scream.

Worthington turned a sickly grey. He put down the sausage he had just speared with his knife.

Girland glanced at Jan and Blanca. Neither of them showed any panic. He put his hand on Mala's and gave it a reassuring pat.

'Think they've spotted us?' Blanca asked her husband.

'No . . . not at the speed they were going.' Jan looked at the fire that was smouldering. 'There's not enough smoke for them to see.' He cut into another sausage. 'Looks as if they are covering the ground by a pattern. Probably, they won't be back this way.'

Worthington pushed aside his plate.

'That's what you say!' His voice was husky with fear. 'How do you know? We must get out of here . . . we're in a trap!'

Girland helped himself to another sausage.

'These aren't bad,' he said, ignoring Worthington. 'They'd be better with a touch of Chili sauce.'

Worthington jumped to his feet.

'Didn't you hear what I said? We are in a trap!'

'I wouldn't have thought so,' Girland said mildly. 'These choppers have a psychological effect . . . they are meant to scare us.' The other three were staring at Worthington as he stood, shaking and frightened. 'Suppose you and I take a look around? We'll go down by the lower plateau. From there we can get a picture of the set-up.' He finished his sausage and his coffee, then got to his feet. 'You others stay under cover. Come on, pal. Let's take a look.'

Worthington hesitated, then as Jan got calmly to his feet and began to collect the empty coffee mugs, seeing Blanca looking away indifferently and Mala staring at him, her dismay at his behaviour plainly showing, he forced himself to follow Girland out of the cabin.

As they moved into the early morning sunshine, they heard the helicopter returning. Worthington was about to dart back into the cabin, but stopped as Girland continued on under the shade of the trees. Shaking, Worthington followed him. The helicopter droned by some three kilometres away.

'He wouldn't still be patrolling if he had spotted us,' Girland said. 'Come on, keep just behind me,' and he started down the long steep descent to the second plateau. As they slid down the path, they saw, from time to time, the other helicopters circling far away to their right and their left. It took them some ten minutes to reach the second plateau that gave them an uninterrupted view of the farm house far below them.

Even Girland was a little startled to see the mass of Army trucks parked in the narrow lane and the activity that was going on around the farm house. He squatted down on his heels, his back against a tree and motioned

Worthington to join him. 'They've certainly called out the troops,' he said.

Worthington looked with horror at the activity below. Even from this distance, he could see the soldiers were all armed with automatic weapons. He felt sweat start out on his face.

'I told you . . . we're in a trap,' he said feverishly. 'We're mad to remain in the cabin. We'll be surrounded.'

Girland began to feel sorry for this weak, frightened man.

'Have you any suggestions what we should do?' he asked quietly. 'Here, have a cigarette. Let's think about it.'

Worthington hesitated, then took the cigarette. His hands were shaking so violently, Girland had to light it for him.

'We must get out!' Worthington said. He took a drag on the cigarette, desperately trying to control his rising panic.

'Yes, but those boys up there would spot us. It's too big a risk to move in daylight.'

'Then we must leave as soon as it is dark! We must! Even then we may be leaving it too late!'

They both heard the approaching beat of the helicopter's engine. It was coming fast. Girland grabbed hold of Worthington and dragged him behind the tree, forcing him flat. The wind rustled the leaves of the trees as the helicopter roared overhead. Dry leaves and sand swirled up in the air from the suction of the propellers.

They lay still side by side, then Worthington said shakily, 'You think I am a coward, don't you? Well, I am. I admit it. It's something I can't do anything about. I would never have become an agent if I thought it would end like this. I needed the money. It seemed so easy. My pupils talked. I have the knack of knowing what is important and what isn't. I was well paid for the information I gave Dorey. I've saved the money. It's in Geneva.' He drew in a shuddering breath. 'I don't think now I'll ever spend it. We're trapped.'

'I wouldn't bet on it,' Girland said cheerfully. 'Those

puppets down there are only kids. We'll get out. We just have to be careful.'

'I have a feeling that I'm not going to get out,' Worthington said. 'There's something I want you to do for me.'

'You'll get out,' Girland said, restraining his impatience with an effort. This man bored him.

'I've left all my money to Mala,' Worthington said. 'If anything does happen to me, will you tell her? It is all arranged. She has only to go to the Credit Suisse Banque at Geneva, prove who she is and then they will give the money to her . . . it is a lot . . . sixty thousand dollars. It's all for her.'

A little startled, Girland looked at him.

'Tell her yourself,' he said. 'Why not?'

'Oh no. She might refuse it,' Worthington said miserably. 'You see, she doesn't love me. I mean nothing to her. It would embarrass her, but when I am dead, she will be glad to have the money . . . then she needn't thank me for it.'

Girland shrugged.

'Don't be so pessimistic. You'll survive.'

Worthington was now watching the activity going on below. He saw Army trucks, loaded with soldiers, driving away to the north.

'I know this district,' he said. 'They are surrounding us. In a couple of hours we will be in a trap. Now's the time to go.'

'On foot?' Girland's question was slightly mocking. 'How far do you imagine we can get in a couple of hours?'

'What are we going to do then?' Worthington asked in despair.

'We'll find a way.' Girland was watching one of the helicopters. It was coming in to land. He watched it disappear behind a line of trees, some twenty kilometres down in the valley from where they were. 'You say you know the district. Did you see where the chopper landed? Do you know how to get there?'

'Yes . . . there's a big field behind those trees. Why?'

'Let's get back,' Girland said and got to his feet. He began to climb to the upper plateau.

122

* * *

Smernoff was enjoying himself. The time was seven minutes to seven and the sun was putting some warmth in him. He had been up all night, but he was used to little sleep. When he hunted, he didn't expect to sleep.

Captain Kuhlan had got his men into position by six o'clock as he had been ordered. Smernoff was surprised that his almost impossible order had been carried out so efficiently. He was now certain his quarries were surrounded. A ring of troops had been made within a thirty kilometre radius of the farm house. He knew it was not possible for them to have walked this distance before the troops had completed their circle. It was now a matter of time before he caught them.

He had had a large breakfast of four eggs, bacon, bread and three cups of coffee. He had bullied Suk. He had praised Kuhlan. Now he was making his way across the dew soaked grass to where a helicopter was standing. The machine had come down to re-fuel and Smernoff decided he would take a ride.

Smernoff believed in surveying the territory where he hunted. He liked riding in a helicopter. He could tell the pilot to pause, and he could lean out of the window and study the ground. A helicopter was the perfect machine for a hunt.

Lieutenant Budovec, the pilot, was waiting patiently by the helicopter. He was short, stocky with dark curly hair, not more than twenty-three years of age, and desperately anxious to impress such an important passenger. He stiffened to attention when Smernoff came over the wet grass, passing two big petrol tankers there to refuel the helicopters.

Smernoff had arranged the refuelling station. He knew the search would be long and tedious. To fly back to the military base, near Prague to refuel, was ridiculous. There must be no delay in this intensive search.

'Well?' he said, pausing before Budovec. 'What news?'

'Nothing so far, Comrade,' Budovec said. He had a map in his hand. 'I have covered this section. Now I intend to

123

cover this one.' His gloved finger traced a small circle on the big scale map.

'I would have thought they would have taken to the hills. You saw nothing suspicious up there?'

'No . . . it is difficult country . . . there are so many trees.'

Smernoff saw Budovec was doubtful.

'But did you see anything at all suspicious?' There was a rasp in his voice.

'Not suspicious, Comrade. There might have been a little smoke up on this hill.' Budovec pointed to the map. 'I circled the spot twice, but decided I had imagined it.'

Smernoff grinned.

'Let us go and look at what you imagined. The slightest clue is important.'

He climbed into the helicopter and settled himself in the passenger's seat. Budovec joined him in the pilot's seat. Smernoff slung the strap of a pair of powerful field glasses round his thick neck.

'Can you remember exactly where you imagined this smoke to be?'

Budovec nodded as he started the engine.

'Yes, Comrade. I remember very well.'

The helicopter took off in a cloud of dust and began its short journey across the valley towards the distant hills.

* * *

'I have an idea,' Girland said. He was sitting on the table, facing the other four. 'It could possibly work out. The helicopters are landing in a field about twenty kilometres from here in the valley. If we could get down there, we might grab one of the machines. I can handle a chopper. There might be a chance that we could cross the frontier, but even if we don't, we can get within easy reach of the frontier . . . what do you think?'

'Of course,' Jan said, excited. 'Twenty kilometres . . . it would take us about two hours . . . it's all down hill. Yes, let's try.'

124

'There are swarms of soldiers . . . I've seen them,' Worthington protested. 'The forest is alive with them.'

Girland took from his pocket the six cartridges which he rolled across the table to Worthington.

'Okay, so there are swarms of soldiers. If we have to, we must fight our way out.'

Worthington stared at him, then aware Mala was watching him, he began to load his gun with an unsteady hand.

Blanca said, 'The helicopters will be guarded. Do you really think it's possible?'

'We can but take a look,' Girland said. 'Two of us have guns. It's worth a try.'

'Listen!' Mala said.

They now became aware of the approaching drone of a helicopter. They remained motionless, listening. The noise became louder and louder and more menacing. The air, stirred by the propellers came into the cabin. The two maps, spread out on the table, took off and flapped against the opposite wall.

The helicopter paused. It seemed to them that it was hovering directly overhead. Everyone in the cabin was tense: Worthington, grey faced. Mala rigid with fear: the Brauns and Girland like stone people. Dust and small stones swirled around, outside the cabin. They could hear the branches of the trees swaying and bending to the suction of the propellers.

Smernoff, leaning out of the window of the helicopter, saw the cabin.

'Lower,' he said.

'It is too dangerous, Comrade,' Budovec returned. 'The trees . . .'

'A little to your right.'

Budovec steered the machine as directed.

Smernoff now could see the cabin clearly through the branches of the trees. His lips parted in a savage smile.

'I think we have them.' He reached for the radio-telephone receiver and gave Suk, waiting anxiously at the farm house, directions. Then nodding to Budovec, he settled back in his seat. Budovec lifted the helicopter and began a wide circling movement around the hill.

'I'll swear that's where they are hiding,' Smernoff said. 'My congratulations, Lieutenant. You have the eyes of a hawk.'

As the helicopter lifted and drifted away, Girland said, 'They've spotted us! We have to move!'

'I told you . . . I've kept telling you,' Worthington exclaimed hysterically. 'We're in a trap!'

Girland smiled at him.

'It's possible, but the trap hasn't been sprung. Let's go!'

Within minutes, they were ready to leave.

'We'll head down the hill towards the landing ground,' Girland said. 'It'll take them a couple of hours to get up here. I'll go first, Jan, you keep close to me, then the girls, then Worthington. Let's move!'

Keeping under the shelter of the trees, conscious of the helicopter circling above, Girland started down the narrow path that led to the second plateau. He moved steadily, remembering Mala. He could have moved much faster, but he knew she wouldn't be able to keep up. The drone of the helicopter's engines above them was a constant reminder that they had to keep under cover.

The helicopter was still circling above them as they reached the lower plateau.

'Wait . . . keep under the trees,' Girland said and moved forward cautiously. He looked down at the distant farm house. Army trucks were coming up the lane, leading to the hill. As he watched, the trucks stopped, unable to go further, and troops holding automatic weapons spilled out. Moving fast, urged on by their officers, they began to climb the hill. Girland attempted to estimate their number. He decided there were well over a hundred of them.

He beckoned to Jan.

'Here they come. We may have to fight our way through them, but no noise. Feel like it?'

Jan nodded. His big fleshy face was grim and his eyes excited.

'Why not?'

Still keeping his voice low, Girland went on, 'It'll have to be the two of us . . . Worthington is useless.'

Again Jan nodded.

126

'Okay, then let's go.' Girland turned to the others. 'Jan and I are going first. Give us three minutes, then come after us. If there is trouble, stop and wait. Okay?'

'Yes,' Blanca said.

Girland looked at Worthington.

'No shooting . . . if they hear shots they'll pinpoint us.'

Worthington, sweating, sickly white, tried to say something, but his voice had gone. He could only nod his head.

Touching Jan's arm, Girland began to slide down the path. It was at this moment Smernoff, high above the hill, spotted Girland through his field glasses.

'There they go!' he exclaimed to Budovec. 'Get lower!' And reaching for the microphone, he relayed to Suk what he had seen. 'Get more men up here! They are coming down. We've got them!'

The helicopter dipped and the trees bent under the air suction. Looking up through the branches, Girland saw the helicopter, hovering just above him. The pilot and the passenger were looking directly at him. He didn't hesitate. His .45 automatic slid into his hand and he fired four shots at the machine. The bang of the gun fire re-echoed in the still air and went crashing down into the valley.

The helicopter swung away. Budovec, hit in the arm, turned the machine towards the landing ground, gritting his teeth, blood running into his glove.

Smernoff cursed.

'Are you badly hurt?' he snarled.

'My arm.' Budovec tried to be heroic, but the pain was making him feel faint. 'I can land.'

'You damn well better land!' Smernoff shouted. 'Get hold of yourself!'

Budovec made the effort and righted the helicopter.

'Well, that's that,' Girland said ruefully as he slid the gun back into its holster. 'If I hadn't got rid of that fly, it would have sat on our tails all the way down. Now, they know we are up here. We must go back. They'll expect us to come down. We'll go up and come down from another direction.'

127

They turned and scrambled up the path where they met the other three coming down.

'We must go back, Girland told them. 'Follow me,' and passing them, he continued up the path. Scrambling, panting and frightened, Worthington and the two girls followed him. Jan brought up the rear. They passed the cabin and then continued up the hill.

Then they heard the sound of an approaching helicopter.

Smerñoff had already alerted Suk to send another machine up to the hill while Budovec was bringing his machine in to land.

The helicopter appeared out of the sun and swooped down on the hill. It was at this moment that the small party were crossing a bare strip of ground, heading towards the shelter of more trees. The soldier, sitting by the pilot, opened up with his automatic rifle. The bullets made puffs of dust within metres of the party. They threw themselves flat. Lying on his back, Girland looked up at the hovering helicopter. He could see the soldier shouting excitedly to the pilot. Girland aimed at the pilot's head and gently squeezed the trigger of his gun. Killed instantly, the pilot slumped forward and the helicopter, out of control, crashed on the hill, turning over and over in a blaze of flame.

'Come on!' Girland exclaimed. 'Fast now!'

They followed him up the hill.

Thick white smoke began to cascade up into the sky from where the helicopter had crashed. The slight wind took the smoke away from them. Girland suddenly stopped. The others crowded around him. He looked at Jan.

'We could have started a forest fire, couldn't we?'

Jan looked at the swirling smoke and nodded.

'Yes . . . listen . . .'

They could hear the roar of the flames, the crackling of burning trees and the smoke was becoming denser. They could also feel the heat of the blaze.

'The wind's taking it down the hill,' Girland said. 'If the

wind changes, we could be in trouble. We'll go down this side of the hill.' He turned to Worthington. 'Give Jan your gun.'

Worthington hesitated, then reluctantly handed the gun to Jan.

'We two go first,' Girland said to Jan. 'Come on.'

As they started down the hill, the smoke swirled overhead. In a few minutes, Girland thought, there would be an umbrella of smoke over the hill, and they would be invisible to the probing eyes of a helicopter pilot. They need not worry about keeping to the trees. They could now take the quickest way down.

The crackling and the roaring of the flames as the flames leapt from one dry tree to another made a terrifying sound. The heat was becoming intense.

Moving fast, leaving the other three well behind, Girland and Jan slid, slithered and ran down the narrow mountain path through the forest, heading towards the valley.

Suddenly Girland pulled up and Jan nearly cannoned into him.

'Listen!'

Faintly above the sound of the forest fire, they could hear the barking of dogs. The two men looked at each other.

'Do you think we are moving right into them?' Jan asked, his face smoke streaked and worried.

'We've got to get down,' Girland said. 'Let's get this organised. I'll go on. You wait here for three minutes, then you come after me. Tell the others also to wait three minutes before coming after you.'

Jan nodded and Girland again started down the path. He was now very alert, his eyes searching the ground ahead of him. There was a lot of cover: big boulders, trees and patches and high grass. It was difficult to get a clear view. He continued on down, gun in hand, aware the barking of dogs was getting nearer.

He finally reached a thick clump of shrubs. He paused. Below him was a road, beyond the road, a forest. He hesitated, then as he was about to slide down the bank to the road, he heard a half-track armoured truck coming up the road. He got behind a tree.

The half-track with four young soldiers, all carrying automatic rifles, sitting in it, chugged by. The sun reflected on their steel helmets. He waited until the half-track continued past, climbing the twisting hill road, then he slid down the bank. He ran across the road and dived down the bank into the forest. He stopped, turned and waited. He could hear another half-track coming up the road. He looked anxiously across the road and saw Jan coming down.

Jan also heard the half-track and he stopped short. Both men, either side of the road, watched the vehicle pass.

Girland climbed back up the bank.

'Stay with the others,' he called. 'See them across. I'll go on.'

Jan nodded.

Girland turned and began the sharp descent through the trees.

Jan waited for the others to join him.

The barking of the dogs grew louder.

As Budovec brought the helicopter to a bumpy landing, and then slumped over the controls, Smernoff opened the cabin door and jumped to the ground.

The three soldiers, guarding the landing ground, came forward at a run. Their young, immature faces were excited.

'Get him out!' Smernoff barked. 'He's hurt.'

Without bothering further about Budovec, Smernoff walked quickly across to where his jeep was waiting.

His stride faltered slightly when he saw Malik standing by the jeep. His dark cruel face tightened, then he joined Malik who was staring up at the hill, watching the helicopter hovering against the blue sky. There came a rattle of automatic weapon fire.

'What do they think they're doing?' Malik rasped. 'Are they firing at them?'

Furious, Smernoff looked skywards. There came a faint

bang of a revolver shot. As the two men watched, the heli-copter heeled out of control and smashed down into the forest. Immediately, there was an explosion, and a moment later part of the forest was in flames.

'Girland!' Malik snarled. 'The fools. Didn't I tell you with Girland you just can't mount a straightforward opera-tion?' He watched the smoke come down in great dark waves, blotting out the forest. 'Now, we have a forest fire. The wind is taking it away from them. Why haven't you caught them before now?'

Smernoff wiped his sweating face.

'It is just a matter of time,' he said. 'We'll catch them. They are surrounded.'

'You should have had them by now!' Malik said in dis-gust. 'Look at that blaze! How can your troops get up there now?'

'Well, Girland and the others can't get down either, so they will have to go down on the other side of the hill,' Smernoff said. 'I have three hundred men there waiting for them . . . men and dogs. It's just a matter of time.'

'Give me a cigarette,' Malik said.

'Here . . . don't you ever smoke your own?'

Malik lit the cigarette and drew smoke into his lungs.

'I don't want them killed,' he said, leaning against the Jeep. 'They must be captured alive.'

'How can we capture a man like Girland alive?' Smer-noff demanded. 'That isn't possible!'

'I want them alive,' Malik said. 'I will make you respon-sible if any of them are killed. I must have them alive. They have information we need.'

'Why didn't you say so before?' Smernoff said, exasper-ated. He ran across to the radio truck, parked under the trees.

Malik again looked at the hill, watching the orange col-oured flames, hearing the crackling of the burning trees, seeing the vast umbrella of smoke and even from where he was standing, feeling the intense heat.

* * *

131

The wind had veered to the south east, and now smoke was beginning to settle over the tree tops, making a curtain of thin mist.

Girland moved silently through the forest, gun in hand, his eyes probing ahead.

He could no longer hear the dogs barking. In the far distance, he could hear the sound of the fire, and the occasional sharp crackle as some dry tree was caught in the approaching flames.

He kept on, seeing the edge of the forest ahead of him and the sunlight, now misty with smoke.

Then he stopped abruptly. He heard voices. He slid behind a tree, listening. A man was saying something in Czech. Satisfied that there was no one in the forest, Girland again moved forward and then saw a steep bank ahead of him that led down into a narrow road. Moving like a ghost, he approached the edge of the forest, and sheltering behind a tree trunk, he looked down onto the road.

A big, covered Army truck was standing by the grass verge. Three soldiers, sweating in the heat, clutching automatic weapons, stood by the truck as their N.C.O. gave them instructions.

Girland surveyed the scene, then moved cautiously back. He saw Jan coming through the forest and he waved to him. Jan joined him.

'There are four men down there,' Girland said, 'and a truck. We can grab the truck, use their uniforms and get to the frontier. What do you think?'

Jan nodded. He pulled Worthington's gun from his hip pocket.

'You'll have to handle it . . . I can't speak the language,' Girland said. 'Put the fear of God into them. They're all young. I'll be covering you.'

Jan nodded again and moved forward. He reached the top of the bank. Girland was right behind him.

They looked at each other, then Girland nodded.

At the top of his voice, Jan yelled, 'Don't move!'

The four men froze. Slowly, the N.C.O. turned his head

132

and looked up at Jan, saw the threatening pistol and turned a whitish green.

'Drop your weapons!' Jan snapped.

The automatic weapons clattered to the ground.

'Turn around! Keep your hands still!'

Mala, Blanca and Worthington now joined them. Girland slid down the bank and collected the rifles which he loaded into the truck.

Jan came down the bank and joined him.

'Tell them to take their uniforms off,' Girland said, stepping back to cover the four men with his gun.

Jan snapped the order. Hurriedly and with panic, the four men stripped off their uniforms and dropped them into the road.

Girland found a coil of rope in the truck. He cut it into lengths. While Jan threatened the four men, Girland tied their hands and legs. Then they lifted each man into the truck.

'Warn them if they make a sound they will be shot,' Girland said and then he beckoned to the two girls and Worthington to come down to the road.

Ten minutes later, Girland and Jan wearing the Czech uniforms, the two girls and Worthington sitting on the floor of the truck, both Blanca and Worthington, guns in hand, the truck moved forward, with Girland at the wheel.

Jan was wearing the N.C.O.'s uniform that scarcely fitted his broad frame. He held an automatic rifle across his thick thighs.

'Now where do we go?' Girland asked.

'First to the left, up the road. Don't drive fast.'

They could hear the helicopter droning overhead.

As they reached the turning and as Girland swung the truck down the long, narrow lane, they saw a Jeep coming fast towards them, sending a cloud of dust behind it.

'Get under cover!' Jan shouted through the rear window.

Hurriedly the two girls and Worthington dragged a tarpaulin that was folded against the side of the truck over them and the four bound soldiers. They lay flat, the tarpaulin covering them.

There was a young, fat officer and two soldiers in the Jeep. The officer waved to Girland and the Jeep stopped. Girland brought the truck to a standstill.

The officer glared at him.

'Where do you think you're going?' he demanded.

Girland had no idea what he was saying. He looked at Jan who leaned across him and made a sloppy salute.

'Orders, Comrade Lieutenant,' he said. 'The divisional commander instructed me to return to headquarters.'

The Lieutenant got out of the Jeep.

Girland thumbed back the safety catch of his revolver. He hid the gun down by his side, his face expressionless.

'Who is your divisional commander?' the Lieutenant barked.

'Colonel Smerzh,' Jan said placidly.

The Lieutenant stepped hurriedly back.

'What are you waiting for?' he exclaimed. 'Get along!'

Girland at Jan's nod, engaged gear and the truck moved past the Jeep.

'Well . . . well . . .' Girland grinned. 'What was it you said?'

Jan told him.

'Smerzh is an important man. I've often seen his photo in the papers. I took a chance.'

'It worked.'

'We have a little less than a hundred kilometres before we reach the frontier,' Jan said. He turned around and called to Blanca. 'You can come out now.' He smiled encouragingly at the girls as they emerged from under the heavy tarpaulin.

Girland slightly increased the speed of the truck. He was feeling more confident. After some thirty minutes of fast driving, they came to a main road.

'Better get under cover again,' he called.

Reluctantly, Blanca pulled the heavy tarpaulin over them.

Once on the main road, they began to pass Army trucks heading in the opposite direction towards the forest fire. Once, a fat, firey-faced Sergeant leaned out of his Jeep, and shouted at them. Girland ignored him and kept on.

Watching in his driving mirror, he saw the Jeep was also keeping on.

A helicopter came low and buzzed them. Jan leaned out of the window and waved. Seeing the steel helmet, the pilot waved back and veered away.

They drove for a further forty kilometres, meeting little military traffic, then rounding a sharp bend, Girland saw a road block ahead. Two half-track armoured cars were across the road. Four soldiers and an N.C.O. were standing in the middle of the road.

'Here's trouble,' Girland said as he slowed the truck. 'I leave it to you.'

Both thumbed back the safety catches on their weapons as the N.C.O., a young, heavily built man came up to the truck.

Jan spoke rapidly to him. Girland had no idea what he was saying, but whatever he said, it had the acquired effect.

The N.C.O. nodded and stepped back. He waved to the soldier sitting in one of the half-tracks who started his engine and moved the vehicle out of the way.

'Go ahead,' Jan said quietly.

Girland engaged gear and moved the truck past the road block, then he accelerated and drove the truck fast down the long, straight road.

'I think we're through now,' Jan said. 'I gave him the same story. This Colonel must be quite a man.'

But he wasn't to know that the N.C.O. reported the movements of every vehicle that passed through the circle that Smernoff had drawn on the map.

Smernoff was sitting at the two-way radio in the farm house, listening in to the reports as they came in. Malik was pacing up and down, his hands clasped behind his back, his face stony and angry.

Voices kept repeating: 'Nothing to report. Smoke making the operation difficult. The dogs are frightened by the fire.' There was a long pause, then a voice came in, 'Division Seven. A truck with two soldiers returning to headquarters, ordered by Colonel Smerzh.'

Smernoff stiffened. He flicked down a switch.

'Division Seven,' he said sharply. 'Repeat your message. Colonel Smerzh is not directing this operation.'

There was a confused pause, then the voice said, 'Repeat: a truck with one N.C.O. and a soldier returning to headquarters, ordered by Colonel Smerzh.'

Smernoff pulled a large scale map towards him.

'Give me the location.'

'Square ten . . . 16.'

Sensing something important was happening, Malik came to stand behind Smernoff as he studied the map.

Smernoff flicked another switch down that brought him in contact with a patrolling helicopter.

'There's a truck heading away from the scene of operation,' Smernoff said. 'Have you seen it?'

'Yes . . . It's heading towards the Austrian border,' the pilot told him. 'It has been checked and passed.'

Smernoff hesitated.

'Stand by,' he said and flicked down another switch that gave him contact with various road blocks.

A voice told him, 'A truck with two soldiers is returning to headquarters by order of Colonel Smerzh. They have passed ten minutes ago.'

Smernoff cursed. He got back to the helicopter.

'Go after that truck! Square ten, 16 or 17,' he shouted. 'Don't lose it! Keep contact and don't fly too close.'

Malik said, 'So they have got beyond your clever barrier, Boris. I will be sorry for you if they get over the frontier.'

'You mean you will be sorry for yourself,' Smernoff said, his face flushed. 'You could never be sorry for anyone except yourself!'

'I think he's got us spotted,' Girland said, raising his voice above the roar of the truck's engine. He was driving fast down a narrow lane, bordered either side by fir trees. Following Jan's directions, he had turned off the main road soon after passing the road block. Now, a helicopter was circling overhead.

'We are within twenty kilometres of the frontier,' Jan said and glanced at his watch. 'We have at least nine hours ahead of us before we can make the attempt to cross. We'd better leave the truck and use the forest path.'

Girland nodded. He could imagine the pilot overhead sending back a stream of radio reports. The net was getting uncomfortably tight.

'Tell me when.' After another five kilometres with the helicopter still overhead, Jan said, 'We're coming to it now. A little bit further . . . now, stop!'

The lane had become even more narrow, and the trees formed a canopy, hiding the truck from the helicopter. Girland pulled up.

As they all descended to the road, Jan said, 'This will have to be fast, and it's going to be rough. They must be after us by now. Follow me.'

He slid down the bank and into the forest. Each of the three men carried an automatic rifle and a rucksack. Blanca had Girland's automatic and a sack of canned food. Mala struggled with the blankets . . . . It was as much as she could manage. They had left Worthington's suitcase in the truck.

Girland kept dropping behind to help Mala, urging her

137

on. He could hear Worthington panting as he forced himself to keep up with Jan's pace.

During the next quarter of an hour, they covered a lot of ground, then they came suddenly on a small, fast moving river.

'We'll use this . . . they are certain to have dogs with them,' Jan said and slid down the bank into the water which came up to his knees. He started downstream, wading forward while the others followed him.

Girland had his arm around Mala and was forcing her along. Worthington began to fall behind. Jan didn't look back. He kept on, knowing time was running out for them.

Very faintly they could hear the barking of dogs. Worthington, gasping, his face white with exhaustion, made an effort and began to catch up with Girland who was having trouble with Mala. She was clinging to him and she would have fallen if he hadn't supported her.

After struggling through the water for a nightmare ten minutes, Jan headed for the bank again and grabbing hold of a tree branch, he hauled himself out on to the bank. He leaned down and helped Blanca out, then Girland passed Mala to him and turned to help Worthington.

They stood on the top of the bank, the trees forming a dense umbrella above them while they listened. They could hear the barking of the dogs, but still in the distance. They could also hear the drone of the helicopter as it circled overhead, vainly trying to find them.

'Not much further,' Jan said, 'then we can rest. Come on!'

He started down a narrow path, then abruptly turned off and plunged through undergrowth. They struggled after him, and after walking for a kilometre or so, Jan waved them to halt.

'There's an airshaft to this mine quite close,' he said. 'It wants some finding. Wait here,' and he moved off into the forest.

Mala dropped to the ground. She felt as if she could never move another step. Worthington too was exhausted and leaned against a tree.

After a five minute wait, Jan returned.

138

'I've found it . . . let's move.'

Girland helped Mala to her feet and the party moved off, following Jan. They came upon a mass of tangled undergrowth to the side of the path. Jan forced his way through, holding back the dead branches and brambles so the girls could follow him. They finally came upon a large hole in the ground.

'This is it. It's not deep,' Jan said, 'and it leads into the mine. I'll go first.' He sat on the edge of the hole, his feet dangling into darkness. 'I'll be at the bottom to catch you as you come,' and he slid out of sight.

A few minutes later, they were all standing in an inky black tunnel that dripped water. Girland lit a candle and they looked around. Mala shivered and put her hand on Girland's arm for comfort.

Lighting another candle, Jan said briskly, 'Follow me and watch your heads.'

Crouching, he started off down the tunnel.

It seemed to Mala they walked for hours then suddenly they came into a vast cave, and Jan thankfully put down his rifle.

'Here we are. We should be safe here for a day or so, then we will make the crossing. It would be too risky to try tonight. Do you agree?'

'I guess so,' Girland said. 'But how do we get out of here?'

'The exit leads right to the frontier,' Jan said and blew out his candle. 'Keep yours alight . . . one is enough.'

Thankfully they sat down on the dry sandy floor of the cave.

'Suppose we have something to eat?' Jan said.

Blanca began to unstrap one of her rucksacks. Girland found a can opener and opened the can of sausages Blanca gave him.

While they were beginning to eat, the pilot of the searching helicopter was radioing back to Smernoff.

Malik was pacing around the room. A radio engineer had rigged up a small loudspeaker so both he and Smernoff could follow the hunt.

The pilot reported that the truck had stopped in a forest

on Map reference 15. Checking his map, Smernoff alerted the nearest patrol.

While waiting for their report, Smernoff leaned back in his chair and lit a cigarette. His face was lined with fatigue. He had been without sleep for thirty-six hours and even his iron constitution was beginning to feel the strain.

Malik came over to the table and stared down at the map.

'They are within ten kilometres of the frontier,' he said.

'Yes.' Smernoff flicked ash onto the floor. 'Suk has moved additional troops there. The whole frontier is alert.' He looked up at Malik. 'You want them alive. This gives them a chance to get across. Remember, my friend, it is your order to capture them alive. This means the guards, even if they see them, can't shoot at them. So . . .'

Malik frowned.

'They have important information.'

Smernoff shrugged.

'They could get across. They now have automatic weapons. What do you expect our men to do if they are shot at? I told you . . . to try to capture Girland alive is impossible. If you think you can take such a risk, then at least, you give me a genuine excuse should I fail to catch them.'

'They must not get across,' Malik said.

'That is different. Then I have your permission to cancel your order to take them alive?'

Malik hesitated. He knew Kovski would engineer his disgrace if he let these people slip through his fingers. He also knew Kovski wanted the information the girl and Worthington had.

'Yes, cancel it,' he said finally. 'They must not get across the frontier.'

'So now we are quite sure of stopping them,' Smernoff said. 'Suk has fifty of the best riflemen at his disposal . . . each equipped with telescopic sights. They are already in position. They cover the whole length of the frontier where these people have to cross. Have a cigarette.' He put his pack of Benson & Hedges on the table. Then picking up the microphone, he began to talk. 'Dead or alive,' he kept repeating. 'Previous instructions cancelled. Repeat: dead or alive.'

As Malik lit the cigarette, he said, 'I'm going out there. I'll take a radio truck and keep in touch with you. Suk is a fool. I don't trust him.'

'Please yourself,' Smernoff said. 'They will probably have them before you get there.'

Malik stared at him and then went out into the warm sunshine. He got in the passenger's seat of the radio truck and told the Sergeant to take him fast to section 15 on his map.

The Sergeant studied the map, nodded and started the engine.

'How long will it take?' Malik demanded.

'Two hours, Comrade . . . the roads are dangerous and narrow.'

'I will give you an hour and a half . . . then, if you are late, you will lose your rank.'

The Sergeant shrugged.

'I would prefer to lose my rank than my life, Comrade.'

Malik smiled. It was not often that he smiled, but he appreciated frankness.

'Very well . . . drive as fast as is safe.'

* * *

Lieutenant Jan Stursa came out of the forest to where Suk was waiting in a Jeep parked off the road.

Stursa was a young, ardent Communist with a growing reputation for ruthless efficiency. Slightly built, fair, thin lipped, he was a man to inspire confidence. He stopped before Suk and saluted smartly.

'Well?' Suk snarled.

He was worried. He knew Malik could have him dismissed. The search had been going on too long now. He couldn't bear to think what failure might mean to him.

'They are somewhere in the forest, Comrade Suk,' Stursa said. 'They can't escape. A battalion of men and dogs have encircled the forest. Now, we are preparing to close in. Within an hour we must have them.'

'Why are you so sure they are here?' Suk demanded.

'They left the truck thirty-five minutes ago. The dogs have picked up their scent but lost it at the river. So we know they entered the forest. My men were already in position beyond the river so they couldn't have gone that way. They haven't come back here. So they must be still there, hiding somewhere.'

'Well, get on with it!' Suk snapped. 'Find them!'

Stursa saluted, then turning, he started back into the forest. He waved to a waiting N.C.O. who began blowing a whistle. Other distant N.C.O.'s hearing the whistle also began to blow their whistles. Then almost shoulder to shoulder, the circle of troops began to move forward.

As Suk watched the beginning of the operation, the N.C.O. in charge of the radio passed the microphone to him. Smernoff told him that Malik was on his way to the scene. Sweating and uneasy, Suk cursed to himself.

'He is wasting his time,' he said into the microphone. 'In less than an hour we will have them . . . they are surrounded.'

'I told him that,' Smernoff said. 'He doesn't believe it. It would be a good thing for you, Comrade Suk, if you did have them by the time he arrives.'

The warning wasn't lost on Suk. He left the radio truck and walked into the forest. Standing on a slight hill, he watched the troops, urged on by Stursa and his N.C.O.'s disappear into the interior.

The forest now became alive with the sound of men moving forward warily. Stursa soon realised that the operation was going to take much longer than an hour. The constant messages coming through the walkie-talkie, alerting him of the progress of his men on the far side of the forest told him how slow the progress was going to be. There was so much undergrowth, so much cover and every metre of the ground had to be checked. Knowing the fugitives were armed, the young soldiers became more and more nervous as the search proceeded.

The N.C.O.'s following behind, cursed them on, confident that they were safe from the first blast of fire should the fugitives appear suddenly from the undergrowth.

Seventy minutes of tenseness dragged by, then Stursa's men reached the river. They paused while Stursa looked across the river at the opposite bank. In a few minutes, he told himself, he should be seeing his troops advancing from the far side of the forest. He could hear them as they came, trampling through the undergrowth. There was no point in crossing the river. Any moment now there must be a cry and a shot to tell him the fugitives had been flushed from their hiding place.

Unable to contain his impatience and uneasiness, Suk had gone into the forest and now joined Stursa.

'What are you waiting for?' he demanded furiously. 'Are you afraid of getting your feet wet?'

'The ring is closed,' Stursa said. His expression was tense and there were sweat beads on his upper lip.

'Closed?' Suk's voice shot up. 'Then where are your prisoners?'

Even as he spoke, he could see the line of advancing troops coming through the trees on the far side of the river.

'Where are they?' he screamed, livid with rage. Then seeing on Stursa's face the admission of defeat, he began to shake his fists at the young Lieutenant. 'You imbecile! I'll have you before the Tribunal!'

Stursa remained stiffly at attention. This was a bitter moment for him. He had been so sure of success.

As Suk continued to scream curses at him, a cold, flat voice said, 'You sound agitated, Comrade Suk.'

Words died on Suk's lips. Blood drained out of his face. He turned to find Malik standing a few yards from him, his green eyes like glass, his face like stone.

'Comrade Malik.' Suk recovered himself and tried to bluster. 'This fool assured me they were in the forest. We have employed nearly five hundred men. Nothing . . . they are not here!'

Malik motioned him to silence. He walked over to Stursa.

143

'Why did you think they were here, Lieutenant?' he asked quietly.

Steadying his voice, Stursa explained.

'The dogs picked up their scent from the truck. They lost it about here,' he said. 'This must prove they entered the forest. They took to the water and the dogs could not follow them. Every metre of the forest has been searched. Somehow—I can't explain it—they have managed to evade the ring I threw around them.'

Malik studied Stursa for a long, searching moment, then he nodded. He liked the look of this young man.

'Could they have found a boat?'

'I have blocked the river at both ends,' Stursa told him. 'They could not pass my men by boat. The river is completely sealed.'

'So?' Malik lit a cigarette. 'You are sure they came into the forest?'

'Yes, Comrade Malik.'

'Yet they have vanished. They are not ghosts. If they are not hiding in the trees, if they are not hiding in the river, if they are not hiding in the forest, then they must be underground. Is there anywhere in this forest where they could go underground . . . a pot hole . . . a cave?'

Stursa shifted uneasily.

'I don't know, Comrade Malik.'

A young N.C.O., listening to all this, came forward and stiffened to attention.

'Permission to speak, Comrade Lieutenant,' he said.

'What is it, Sergeant?' Malik asked.

'There is an air shaft not far from here, leading to a disused copper mine. I used to play in the mine when I was a boy,' the Sergeant said, staring above Malik's head, his face dripping with the sweat of embarrassment.

'Can you take us to this air shaft?' Malik asked.

'I think so, Comrade. It is some years since I was there, but I think I can find it.'

Malik turned to Suk.

'Tell Smernoff what is happening. You need not come with us.' Turning his back on Suk, he signalled to Stursa to follow him. 'Lead the way, Sergeant.'

The Sergeant started off along the river bank with Malik and Stursa following him.

Suk watched them go, knowing his small reign of power was now over.

* * *

Girland sat with his back against the slope of the cave with Jan by his side. The two girls and Worthington were sleeping. In the light of the candle, Jan was drawing a map of the mine in the hard sand.

'This is a bad place to get lost in,' he said. 'This tunnel to your right leads down to the mine and it is full of water. This tunnel to your left eventually leads to an exit that comes out into the middle of the mine field, guarding the frontier. At least, by using this route, we by-pass the seed bed and the first alarm fence. The mines are buried about ten centimetres deep. They have vibration fuses. It takes quite a lot of vibration to set them off. My friend started the crossing at eight o'clock. It was dark. It took him four hours, moving centimetre by centimetre on his stomach. He must have passed over several mines, but by moving so slowly and gently, he survived.' Jan looked up and rubbed his stubbly jaw. 'We are five. This makes the operation five times more difficult and five times more dangerous. Two of us must go the first night, two the second and then the final one. I go with my wife. I leave it to you if you are the last or Worthington is. I should have thought Worthington should be the last. You could control the girl if she panics. Worthington couldn't.'

Girland nodded.

'There is a fence . . . a double electrified fence, but there is also an underground stream flowing under the fences so the ground is soft. It is possible, by lying completely flat on this sodden ground to get under the bottom wire. The ground sinks under your weight. If you touch the bottom wire, you will, of course, be electrocuted.'

Girland grimaced.

'It sounds marvellous, and how about the Watch Towers?'

145

'The nearest one to where we cross is a hundred metres. That is to your right. To your left there is another tower three hundred metres away. The revolving searchlights from the two towers don't quite meet, and it is through this narrow lane of shadow that we will have to move.' Jan shrugged and lit a cigarette from the candle flame. 'I told you we could get through only if we have lots of luck . . . we'll need lots of luck.'

'Yes.' Girland studied the map of the mine and then began to rub it out, smoothing the sand with the flat of his hand.

'Even when we are across the frontier, the guards in the towers, if they spot us, will fire at us as long as we are within range. There is no question of standing up and running for it. You will have to crawl for at least six hundred metres to where there is enough cover to stand up and run.'

'Heck!' Girland exclaimed. 'It sounds quite an operation.'

'It can be done. I've seen it done.'

'If one of us makes a mistake, then we're all finished. The crossing will be spotted.' Girland looked thoughtfully at Jan. 'I must go first, Jan. I have a Top Secret document that must get back to Paris. I'm sorry, but this document is so explosive, I must get it back.'

'No document, however explosive, is more important than my wife's life,' Jan said, his fleshy face hardening. 'No . . . we have brought you here . . . we go first.'

'If you touch off a mine, then I don't get this document out,' Girland said. 'I assure you it is more important than your wife. I'm sorry, but that's the way it is.'

'My wife and I go first,' Jan said. 'I'm sorry too. I know where to cross . . . you don't. If we don't go first, none of us goes!'

'Suppose we toss for it?' Girland suggested, always willing to back his luck.

'I don't toss for my wife's life,' Jan said coldly. 'We go first or none of us goes!'

Girland studied the hard, fleshy face. There was no compromise in Jan's expression. Girland didn't blame him.

146

He would have done the same if he had been married to a woman like Blanca.

'Okay, you win . . . so you go first.'

'Yes,' Jan said. 'Now I'll get some sleep. We go tomorrow night. Then you and the girl the following night . . . then Worthington.'

Worthington, awake, had been listening to the whispered conversation. He started up, threatening the two men with his gun. 'No! I heard what you were saying. I'm not crossing on my own! Do you hear? I won't do it!'

Girland looked at him with resigned boredom.

'What a pest you are,' he said. 'Put that gun down and for God's sake, go to sleep!'

'No! You will go first. I will go with you,' Worthintgon said. 'I must get out. Mala can come after us. These small time farmers . . .'

'Shut up . . . listen!' Girland said sharply. The snap in his voice stilled Worthington.

They remained motionless. Very faintly, coming down the long tunnel, they could hear voices.

Snatching up an automatic rifle, Girland left the cave and began moving fast and silently up the tunnel to the air shaft. As he approached the shaft, he heard voices distinctly.

It was at this moment that Malik, Stursa and the Sergeant had reached the hole, leading down into the mine.

'This is it, Comrade,' the Sergeant said.

'Where does it lead to?' Malik asked.

'There is a long tunnel, then a cave,' the Sergeant told him. 'From the cave there are two other tunnels. I don't know where they lead to.'

'Are there other exits?'. Malik asked, his voice coming clearly to Girland as he squatted in the tunnel. Malik was speaking German.

'I don't know. When I was a small boy . . .'

'Never mind about your boyhood,' Stursa snapped. 'I will go down and find out.'

'Wait,' Malik said. 'If they are down there, you should not go. One of them is highly dangerous. No . . . we don't go down. We will drop a tear gas bomb down there

147

and then your men, with gas masks, can go down and see what there is to see.'

'We have no tear gas bombs,' Stursa said impatiently. 'I am going down.' He had three hand grenades hanging from his belt. He unhooked one. 'This is my operation, Comrade Malik. I give orders here.'

Listening to this, Girland turned and sped back down the tunnel. He reached the cave.

'Quick! They are coming down,' he said. Already the two girls were awake and getting to their feet. 'Get up the tunnel to the frontier!'

Turning, he ran back up the tunnel while Jan, grabbing up two of the rucksacks, herded the girls towards the left hand tunnel.

Left on his own, Worthington hesitated. Ever since he had left his home, he had felt he had no future. Now, suddenly, he had a compulsive urge finally to prove to himself that he wasn't the weakling he knew they all thought he was. He followed Girland back up the tunnel.

Hearing him, Girland paused and waved him back.

'I can handle this. Follow the others!'

'No! I can help you!' Worthington said desperately. He could just make out Girland's silhouette from the light coming down the air shaft.

'Get the hell out of here!' Girland snapped and then started off to the tunnel again.

Worthington hesitated. He was terrified, but now, he was like a man biting down on an aching tooth. He had to prove to himself that he was as good a man as Girland. If he didn't, he knew he had no hope with Mala, and she was his only desire for survival. He gave Girland a moment or so to reach the air shaft, then he slowly walked up the tunnel, sweat dripping down his face, his hand gripping his gun so tightly, cramp set up in his arm.

Stursa came into the tunnel with a rush, skidded, landed on his back, then scrambled to his feet.

Girland was in the dark shadows, leaning against the wall of the tunnel. Stursa didn't see him, but he did see the crouching outline of Worthington as he came slowly and cautiously towards him. Worthington saw him, jerked up his gun and fired. The bang of the gun was like a clap of thunder in the confined space. As Stursa fell, he manged to throw the grenade. It hit Worthington on his chest, then dropped to the floor of the tunnel. Worthington fell flat on it, not knowing what it was, only desperate to get under cover. The grenade exploded. Girland felt wet stickiness hit his face. Some of the roof of the tunnel came down, showering him with sand and stones.

The noise of the exploding grenade deafened and shocked him. For some moments he remained limply against the wall of the tunnel, then making the effort, he went over to Stursa who was bleeding and unconscious. His groping hands found the two other hand grenades and he quickly unhooked them from Stursa's belt. Then he ran down the tunnel to where Worthington was lying. He flicked his cigarette lighter alight, peered at Worthington, grimaced and then ran back to the cave. Worthington was a jelly of blood and smashed bone, held together only by his clothes.

As Girland entered the cave, Jan came down the tunnel, gun in hand.

'Worthington's dead,' Girland said. 'Get back up the tunnel!'

'You all right?' '

'Yes. Get going!'

Jan went back and Girland heard more rock falling in the tunnel leading to the air shaft. He pulled the pin from one of the grenades, then tossed the grenade in an underhand, looping throw down the tunnel.

The explosion brought down another fall of stones. He pulled the pin from the second grenade and threw it down the tunnel.

The thunder of the explosion and the crash of falling stones told him that the tunnel was now sealed, but to be certain, he lit a candle and walked up the tunnel. The smoke, dust and falling stones made an impassable barrier. Gasping for breath, he started back, crossed the cave and ran up the tunnel where Jan was waiting.

'What's happening?' Jan demanded, holding aloft a

lighted candle while he stared at Girland who was smothered with dust and spotted with Worthington's blood.

'I've blocked the tunnel. It could take them some time to get through . . .' He stopped short as there came a tremendous crash of falling rock and dust swirled up the tunnel, making them cough. Girland heard Mala scream as the dust swirled past her.

'Sounds as if the cave's gone,' he said. 'They might think we're buried.' Pushing past Jan, he went on up the tunnel to where the two girls were crouching in the darkness.

Malik drew back from the hole as the first grenade exploded. He saw dust and smoke rush out of the air shaft and the noise of the exploding grenade set his teeth on edge.

'The fool!' he said viciously. 'What does he think he is doing?'

The Sergeant stood by helplessly. Malik waited, listening. Then the other two grenades exploded and he could hear the crashing of falling rocks.

He whirled around to the Sergeant.

'Get men! Quickly!'

The Sergeant dashed away while Malik watched the dust rising out of the hole. He listened to the rumbling sound as rocks continued to fall, and he grimaced. By using his grenades, Malik reasoned, the fool had collapsed the tunnel.

But did this mean the fugitives were buried? Were there other exits from the mine. There must be . . . but who knew about them? Malik realised he was wasting time standing by the air shaft. He must alert Smernoff.

He started after the Sergeant, running with long strides, brushing through the undergrowth. Half-way back to the radio truck, he met the Sergeant with five, scared looking soldiers.

'Guard the air shaft,' Malik. said, stopping. 'Don't go down. Stay there,' and then he continued on his way back to the radio truck.

It took him more than twenty minutes before he was talking to Smernoff over the radio telephone. Briefly, he explained the situation.

'Find someone who knows about this mine,' Malik said. 'There must be a map of it somewhere. There are certain to be other exits. Send men with gas masks. I want them down the air shaft to see what has happened. Send an ambulance!'

'Yes, but all this will take time,' Smernoff said calmly.

'Hurry!' Malik snarled and cut the connection.

* * *

It seemed to Mala they had been walking hundreds of kilometres as she staggered along the tunnel. Jan, holding a flickering candle, went first, Blanca behind him, then Mala with Girland just behind her.

Mala couldn't believe that Worthington was dead. She was in a state of shock. If it hadn't been for Girland's hand on her arm, giving her assurance, she would have flopped down and wept her heart out.

Jan knew he was driving the two girls too hard, and after ten minutes of fast walking, he stopped.

'Let's rest for a moment,' he said. 'We have about four more kilometres to go.'

Gratefully, the two girls dropped to the ground.

Girland and Jan squatted on their heels. The air in the tunnel was bad, and they all had difficulty in breathing.

'We must now cross the frontier tonight,' Jan said. Peering at his watch in the dim light, he went on, 'We should get to the exit in another two hours. It will be dark enough. Blanca and I go first. The frontier guards will be alert, but we can't afford to wait. It won't take them long to break through into the cave and then they will come after us.'

'Are there any other exits?' Girland asked.

'This is the only possible exit,' Jan told him. 'The other one from the right hand tunnel leads under the frontier and the exit comes out in Austria, but there is water in the tunnel. You can't get through. We have tried. It means swimming through the tunnel that is four kilometres long. The water is oily and stagnant. You can't breathe. It is impossible.'

151

'You mean the right hand tunnel leads directly into Austria?' Girland asked, his voice sharpening.

'Yes, but that means nothing. No one can swim in that water and stay alive. There are escaping gases. The water is frightful . . . oil, filth and then there are water rats. It is wasting time even to think of escaping that way.'

'You are sure about this?'

'Of course I'm sure,' Jan said curtly. 'Do you think we haven't tried? This is a direct access to the Austrian frontier. Last year, I lost a good friend who took the risk rather than face the minefield. His body floated back.' He grimaced. 'Covered in oil, bloated and half eaten by rats. That way is impossible.' He stood up. 'We had better get moving again.'

They started off, moving more slowly, aware that the ground was rising. Every half hour, they stopped to rest for ten minutes, then they continued on again. By now Girland had his arm around Mala, supporting her. She was crying, dragging one foot after the other, scarcely conscious.

Malik had returned to the air shaft. He found the Sergeant and the five soldiers sitting on a fallen tree, anxiously staring at the hole that led to the mine, their rifles at the alert.

The dust and smoke no longer drifted from the hole and Malik went to the hole and knelt down, flashing the powerful beam of a flashlight he had brought with him from the radio truck into the mouth of the tunnel.

The air in the tunnel seemed to have cleared, but he saw no reason why he should risk his life which he valued. He stood up and beckoned to the young Sergeant.

'Here, take this flashlight and go down,' he said.

The Sergeant took the flashlight and without hesitation, lowered himself down the air shaft, hung for a moment, then slid down into the tunnel.

Malik waited impatiently. Several minutes crawled by, then the Sergeant appeared at the bottom of the air shaft. He seemed shocked, his eyes very wide, his face white.

'The Lieutenant is dead,' he announced.

Malik knelt at the top of the hole.

'Never mind about the Lieutenant,' he snapped. 'What's happened to the tunnel?'

'It is completely blocked.'

'What is the air like down there?'

'It is all right.'

Malik hesitated, then swinging his feet down into the hole, he joined the Sergeant.

'There is another man down here, Comrade Malik,' the Sergeant said. 'The grenade has killed him.'

Malik walked over to Worthington's body, swung the beam of his flashlight on Worthington's dead face. Then he walked a few steps to examine the blocked tunnel. Piles of rock and sand had formed a solid wall. Even as he was examining this obstruction, he could hear rocks thudding down somewhere behind the wall. He cursed under his breath. Had the fugitives been buried? he wondered. He could not afford to take chances. He must find out if there were any other exits from the mine.

Three soldiers, lying flat, hauled him up from the air shaft and then they brought up the Sergeant.

'Stay here,' Malik said. 'There is an ambulance coming,' and he strode off in the gathering dusk to the radio truck.

Back at the farm house, Smernoff was snarling over the telephone to an official of the Ministry of Mines whom he had traced to his two room apartment. The official told him it was possible that there was a map of the disused mine, but this could not be found until the following morning. The Ministry was closed.

'I want it immediately!' Smernoff barked. 'Do you understand? Immediately!'

'It is impossible, Comrade,' the official stammered.

'Nothing is impossible! I am now returning to Prague. If the map is not waiting for me at the Ministry by the time I arrive, you will suffer!' Smernoff yelled. 'This is an affair of State! I want that map and I intend to have it!' He slammed down the receiver.

In the tunnel, Jan was consulting his watch.

'It is after nine,' he said. 'It will be dark enough. We have only a few metres before we come to the exit.'

They were grouped together at the end of the tunnel.

153

The opening was overgrown by shrubs and trees. The cool night air came to them, fanning their heated faces.

'It'll take us at least four hours to cross the minefield. You could still have time to follow us,' Jan said. 'I've told you what to expect. You must go slow . . . and I mean slow. If you move a metre in five minutes, you should be safe. Do you understand?'

'Yes,' Girland said.

'You will watch us cross. You will see our direction. Follow that and it will bring you to the soft ground, so you can get under the wire. Be very careful going under the wire. If you touch it, you will die. You understand?'

'Yes,' Girland repeated.

'All right, then we will go.' Jan smiled at him and offered his hand. 'Good luck.'

Girland gripped his hand.

'And good luck to you.'

The two girls kissed. Mala was shaking with nerves. Blanca touched her hair softly.

'Don't be frightened. He'll look after you. He is like my man,' she said quietly.

Jan put his hand on Blanca's shoulder and she left Mala and followed him to the mouth of the tunnel.

Mala shuddered and turned to Garland. He put his arm around her, holding her close to him.

'This is going to be a terrific story to tell your grandchildren,' he said. 'You will bore them to tears.'

'I don't want grandchildren! I'm frightened,' Mala wailed.

'You can't be frightened with me around,' Girland said, and pulling her against him, his lips found hers.

Mala strained wildly against him, her hands sliding down his broad back, then Girland pulled away, took her hand and led her to the entrance of the tunnel.

Jan and Blanca had got through the undergrowth, covering the exit of the tunnel. They were squatting on their heels, examining the innocent looking strip of thick grass that separated the distance to the high electrified fence.

Girland and Mala joined them.

Every two minutes two blades of light from the watch

154

tower searchlights swept the ground. The two lights did not quite meet, leaving a narrow lane of ground unlit.

Jan said quietly, 'That's the way we'll go.' He had shed his rucksack and rifle. He spoke to his wife in rapid Czech. They looked at each other and smiled. Then they kissed. 'So long,' Jan said, turning to Girland. 'We meet again in Austria.'

The two men gripped hands, then sliding flat, Jan began to move out into the open. Blanca, white faced, tense, managed a smile at Mala, then she began to crawl into the open behind her husband.

Girland found he was sweating. Mala put her hand in his. He could feel she was trembling. He pulled her against him, his arm going around her.

Centimetre by centimetre, Jan and Blanca moved on. Every time the blades of the searchlights revolved near them, they remained motionless, then as the lights moved away, they continued the snail-like crawl.

The tension was unbearable. Even Girland's iron nerves were strained. Mala couldn't bring herself to watch any more. She clung to Girland, her face buried against his shoulder.

Girland thought: I wonder if I'll get her across? Suppose she panics. She could do. I'll have to take her by my side. She won't follow me. I can't trust her to go first. I have a problem here.

He could still see the other two as they crept with infinite care across the deadly grass. They had only covered ten metres, probably less. Girland longed for a cigarette, but he realised it would be too dangerous to strike a light.

Minutes crawled by.

'They're going fine,' Girland said, holding Mala against him. 'Relax . . . they still have a long way to go . . .'

Then something happened. Girland was never to know exactly what did happen. It was possible that Jan, dragging himself forward on his elbows, came into direct contact with a hidden mine.

There was a blinding flash and a bang. Jan's body was flung up in the air and fell with a sickening thump some metres away and another mine exploded.

Mala screamed.

Girland held on to her, his mouth dry, his heart hammering.

Blanca jumped to her feet and was running frantically towards Jan when machine guns opened up from the two watch towers.

Girland saw her caught in a stream of bullets. She reared back and more bullets slammed into her, then she fell and another mine exploded.

The whole section of the frontier erupted into a blazing, nerve shattering roar as machine gun bullets churned up the ground, kicking up a curtain of dust and flying grass.

A siren began to wail, and the night became hideous with the noise of violence.

chapter eight

For the past hour, Malik had been sitting in the radio truck waiting and seething with fury. Next to him sat a Sergeant Radio Engineer, listening through headphones to a flood of messages coming to the truck. So far nothing of importance had come through. An officer at the farm house had, sent a message to say that Smernoff had returned to Prague. Malik guessed Smernoff had gone after a map of the mine. In the meantime, he had to contain his impatience.

As he was lighting a cigarette, he heard in the far distance a dull thump of an explosion. Then another. Then faint sounds of machine gunfire. He stiffened to attention and looked at the Sergeant who was sitting forward, listening.

There was a long pause, then the Sergeant said something in Czech into the microphone strapped to his chest. He listened. Again he said something, then taking off his headphones, he turned to Malik, his face showing his excitement.

'There has been an attempt to cross the frontier, Comrade Malik,' he said. 'A man and a woman have been killed by a mine. An investigation is now taking place.'

Girland? Malik wondered.

'I want a description of those two!' he said. 'Get it!'

The Sergeant replaced his headphones. He flicked switches on his radio set, frowned, flicked more switches, waited, then shook his head.

'They have gone off the air, Comrade,' he said finally.

'Keep trying!'

157

'A message coming in. Comrade Smernoff to Comrade Malik,' the Sergeant said. 'He wants to talk to you,' and he passed the headphones and the microphone to Malik.

'Boris?'

'Yes. I have a map of the mine. There are only two exits. One of them is completely blocked with water . . . the other leads directly to the minefield at the frontier.'

'They have already tried to cross. Two of them are dead,' Malik said. 'Are you sure the second exit is blocked?'

'Yes . . . the tunnel is full of water.'

Malik thought for a brief moment.

'Come here and bring the map,' he said and handed back the headphones and the microphone to the Sergeant. 'See if you can find out who these two dead are.'

The Sergeant juggled with switches. After a few moments, he got a reply. Turning to Malik he said, 'The bodies are in the middle of the minefield. It will take some time to get to them. From what can be seen through field glasses, the man is heavily built and the woman is blonde.'

Could it be Girland? Malik wondered. But if Girland was still alive, would he attempt to reach the Austrian frontier by the second exit? Smernoff had said the exit was blocked by water. Did that mean Girland couldn't break out? Was he trapped in the mine?

There was nothing to do but to wait for Smernoff to arrive.

'Ask them how long it will take to clear the minefield,' Malik said.

The Sergeant again made contact with one of the watch towers. After some moments of talking, he said to Malik, 'About five hours. They have no mine detectors. These are coming. The clearance will be dangerous and slow.'

Malik had some experience of frontier hazards. The possible delay came as no surprise. Five hours! If Girland was alive, he could do a lot in that time. He might even escape!

He got out of the truck and began to pace up and down the narrow lane, smoking cigarette after cigarette.

Smernoff arrived two hours later. He had been driving

like a lunatic and twice he had nearly skidded into a ditch. Even Malik was startled to see him so soon. He had thought Smernoff couldn't possibly have made the journey under two and a half hours.

'Let me see the map,' Malik said, striding to Smernoff's dusty car as Smernoff got out.

Smernoff handed him the map. Using his flashlight and spreading the map on the hot hood of the car, Malik examined it.

'There are two exits. You see this second one comes out three hundred metres inside the Austrian border. But I am told it is completely blocked.' Smernoff indicated on the map the two exits.

'What does that mean . . . completely blocked?' Malik demanded.

'There is water in the tunnel for at least four kilometres.'

'Girland would think nothing of swimming four kilometres!'

Smernoff grinned.

'The water is stagnant, oily and full of water rats. They would eat him alive. Besides, there is a concentration of gas in the tunnel.'

'How do you know?' Malik snapped.

'They made a test six months ago. The gas is lethal.'

'It could have evaporated by now.'

Smernoff shrugged.

'Experts have told me the tunnel is impassable. You either believe them or you don't.'

'If we were dealing with anyone but Girland, I would believe it. Girland is different. If there is the slightest chance of escaping, he will escape.'

'So what are you going to do?'

Malik moved away from the car while he thought. Then he returned and studied the map.

'The second exit is here,' he said, putting his thick finger on the map. 'That is where I'm going to be when—if—he comes out.'

Smernoff stared at him.

'Are you mad? You can't touch him in Austria!'

159

'I can wait by the exit . . . it is only three hundred metres from the frontier. If he comes out, I will kill him. Before the Austrian guards arrive, I'll be back this side.'

'It's madness!'

'Girland is not to escape!'

Smernoff hesitated, then shrugged.

'Very well. Then I'll come with you.'

'No. You must stay on this side. When you hear shooting, you must organise my return. The electricity must be cut off. A path must be made for me through the minefield. I don't trust these fools to do the job properly. You must see to it.'

'You don't even know Girland will come out by this second exit,' Smernoff pointed out. 'You could be risking your life for nothing.'

'That is a chance I am prepared to take. If he doesn't break out, then he will be trapped in the mine. As soon as the minefield has been cleared, we send troops into the mine. But I am taking no chances. Now we will go to the frontier post where the bodies are. We're wasting time here.'

He slid under the wheel of Smernoff's car and started the engine, Smernoff got in beside him.

The car shot away down the narrow lane, leaving a cloud of dust behind it.

*   *   *

Girland wondered how long it would be before the exit from the mine would be discovered and they would have soldiers after them. He thought their chances of survival were slight, but such was his nature, he never considered defeat. If he was alone, he thought, he could cope with the situation, but to be burdened by this hysterical, sobbing girl, made his task trebly difficult.

They were still at the mouth of the tunnel, listening to the gun fire and watching the searchlights darting like snakes' tongues over the bullet shattered ground.

Mala was staring with horror at the two lifeless bodies and crying.

160

Girland stood up and taking hold of her, pulled her to her feet. She collapsed against him.

'Stop it!' he said sharply. 'Stop being a weakling! Do you hear me?'

She clung to him, her body shaking, her breath coming in short gasps. He shoved her roughly away. She staggered back against the wall of the tunnel, then deliberately and hard, he slapped her face.

Mala caught her breath, stiffened, then as she opened her mouth to scream, he slapped her again, this time so hard she slid down the wall and landed in a heap on the sandy ground. He dragged her upright.

'Better?' He put his arms around her. 'Come on, baby. Get hold of yourself. I'll help you if you'll help yourself.'

She broke away from him.

'You hurt me! Oh! You hurt me!'

Girland smiled at her.

'You had to be hurt. You were behaving like a five-year-old.'

She swung her open hand. Girland saw the blow coming, but he made no attempt to avoid it. Her open palm smacked against the side of his face with considerable force. He remained still, watching her.

'Go ahead . . . do it again if it's fun,' he said quietly.

She looked at him, then he saw in the reflected light from the searchlights, life come into her eyes.

'I'm sorry,' she said. 'I didn't mean to do that. You just got me mad,' and moving up to him, she kissed his cheek. 'Forgive me?'

'Of course.'

'What are we going to do?'

Girland drew in a sigh of relief. Well, at least, that was the first problem out of the way.

'We're going to get out of here. It'll be tough, but we'll do it. We're going for the Austrian tunnel.' He pulled her against him and kissed her, his lips hard on hers. 'In three days from now, I'll buy you the best and most expensive dinner Paris can give us.'

She regarded him and forced a smile.

'It's a date,' she said.

They started down the tunnel. Girland carried an automatic rifle and a rucksack while Mala held the lighted candle. It took them over an hour to reach the junction of the two tunnels. The further they walked, the worse the air became. Soon both were breathing with difficulty. Girland had long discarded his jacket, now he threw off his shirt, Mala walked in her jeans and bras. She had taken off her sweater.

~~Here~~ we are,' Girland said breathlessly. 'We turn right and start again. How are you doing?'

'I'm managing,' she returned, 'but I can't stand these any more,' and zipping down her jeans, she dragged them off her sweating legs.

His eyes ran over her trim figure. She looked at him.

'Go on . . . look! I hope I please you.'

He smiled at her.

'You're lovely. In three days' time, we are going to make wonderful love together. Is that another date?'

She nodded.

'Yes . . . it's another date.'

They started up the second tunnel. The air seemed a little fresher and they were able to move faster. After some two kilometres, Mala paused.

'Could we rest? I'm nearly flat out.'

'Sure,' Girland said. He took the candle from her and dropped the rifle and the rucksack on the ground. 'You take a rest. You've earned it. I'm going to look around.'

'Don't leave me!'

'Come on, baby!' Girland said sharply. 'You're doing fine. I won't be a couple of minutes.'

'Please . . .' She was now lying on the sandy floor of the tunnel, looking pleadingly up at him. The candlelight made shadows around her. Her hand moved behind her back. The bras slid off. 'Put the candle out . . . please take me.'

He realised her necessity and was violently stirred. He blew out the candle and came down beside her. As his arms slid around her, she moaned, her mouth seeking his. His thrust into her made her cry out, then she gripped him

162

in her arms, holding him fiercely, her long legs twining around his, her cooling body arching to his.

Time stood still for them. The danger, the frontier, the tunnel became distant nightmares. Both of them drifted away into an ecstasy of mutual pleasure. During that all too brief period they left the world and orbited into that special space reserved only for proficient lovers.

Girland was the first to return to reality. Very gently, he released himself from Mala and turned on his side. His hands still moved caressingly down her slim back. She remained still, breathing in slow, gasping breaths, now relaxed and satisfied.

He listened to the sound of water. His mind switched from the pleasure he had had from her to the task ahead of them.

'Stay still, honey,' he said. 'Wait for me.'

He moved away from her and stood up.

'Don't leave me,' she murmured, trying to hold on to him.

He pushed her hands away.

'Stay still.' He slid into his trousers, then groped for the candle. He lit it and began walking up the tunnel.

'Mark!'

'I'll be back . . . stay where you are.'

As he moved up the tunnel, he became aware of a rank smell. He kept on, then paused as he saw five or six oil drums standing against the wall of the tunnel. He tilted one. It moved easily . . . it was empty. He paused to think. An oil drum would float, he reasoned. This could be a way of getting through the tunnel of water ahead of them.

He heard Mala coming down the tunnel and he waited for her. She arrived, dragging the rifle and the rucksack.

'I couldn't bear to be alone,' she said. 'I'm sorry.'

'Look at these. We might make a raft. Three of them together. Let's see where the water is.'

Putting his arm around her and holding the flickering flame of the candle high, he continued up the tunnel. They didn't have to walk far before they came to an abrupt stop. The floor of the tunnel slid down abruptly for some three metres and below was black, oily water. The smell from the water sickened them both.

'We can't go this way!' Mala exclaimed, recoiling. 'We can't!'

'This is the way, honey, and this is the way we're going.' He put down the rifle and rucksack. He rummaged in the rucksack and found another candle and lit it.

Then giving her the candle and taking the other one, he returned to the oil drums. He pulled one of them on its side and rolled it up the tunnel to the water's edge. Mala followed him, now holding both candles. They returned for the second drum. As Girland moved it, there came a sudden flurry and something streaked over his foot and disappeared into the darkness. Mala screamed and dropped one of the candles, backing away.

'It was a rat!' she cried, shuddering.

'Well, it's gone now,' Girland said and picked up the candle. He relit it from the other she was holding in her shaking hand. 'Now don't go temperamental on me, baby. I need your help.' He turned up the second drum. 'You wait here. I'll be right back for the third one.'

'I'm keeping with you!' Mala said. 'Do you think there are any more rats?' She looked fearfully into the darkness.

'I shouldn't think so,' Girland lied, remembering what Jan had told him. He saw no point in telling her the truth. She was frightened enough as it was.

He rolled the drum up the tunnel and stood it by the first drum. Mala kept close to him. They returned for the third drum. As he shifted it, he saw behind it something that looked like a snake. He controlled the impulse to jump back and standing motionless, he said quietly, 'Give me a candle.' The tenseness in his voice made Mala stiffen with terror. She gave him a candle. Holding the flickering flame high, he looked at the snake-like thing. It was a coil of rope.

'Luck's coming our way,' he said and reached down and picked up the rope. An enormous spider lay under the rope. It scuttled away into the darkness, passing close to Mala who caught a glimpse of it. She jumped back, catching her breath, sickened at the sight of its obscene, hairy legs.

'Only a spider,' Girland said. 'You're a big girl now. Here . . . take the rope. I'll handle the drum.' As he handed her the coil of rope, he smiled at her. 'Don't forget, we have a date: the best and the most expensive dinner in Paris.'

'I'm not forgetting,' she said and taking the coil of rope, she hung it over her shoulder.

'That's my girl . . . come on,' and Girland began rolling the third drum up the tunnel.

* * *

Malik lowered his field glasses.

'That's not Girland,' he said in disgust. 'So he's still in the mine!'

He was standing with Smernoff at the foot of one of the watch towers, surveying the minefield where three soldiers were cautiously sweeping the ground with mine detectors. 'I must get across. I can't wait for them to lift the mines.' He turned to the Major in charge of the frontier post, a short, fat man who had arrived from the Police Control Post by fast car. 'Have the electricity cut off!' he snapped. 'I must get across. Get trestle tables from somewhere. If they are put across the ground, I should be able to walk over.'

The fat Major looked startled.

'Not if the legs of the tables happen to touch a mine, Comrade,' he said. 'It is far too dangerous. It would be possible and much safer to use a rope with a hook. If you could swing yourself across . . .'

Malik looked across the minefield, then nodded.

'Yes . . . arrange it.'

As the Major hurried off, Smernoff said, 'You are being stupid. Girland may not come out of the mine. If the rope breaks . . .'

'I am going across,' Malik said. 'Oblige me by keeping quiet!'

Smernoff shrugged. He produced his pack of Benson &

Hedges and offered it. Malik took a cigarette and both men lit up.

'I need an automatic pistol,' Malik said, letting smoke drift down his wide nostrils.

'There is one in the truck.'

'Good. From here to the second exit is three kilometres. I will cross here and walk by the wire. I will return the same way. See these fools clear a path through this minefield by the time I return.'

'I'll get the pistol,' Smernoff said and hurried away to the radio truck. He found an automatic pistol in one of the lockers, checked that it was loaded, then came back to where Malik was now talking to the Major who had returned.

'It is loaded and in order,' Smernoff said, handing the pistol to Malik.

Malik nodded and turned back to the Major who was saying, 'They are splicing a hook to a rope now. It won't take long. The electricity has been cut.'

Malik looked at his watch. He reckoned, once he was across the fence, it would take him under an hour to reach the second exit. Girland had been down in the mine now for three hours. He couldn't swim four kilometres under two hours—even if he managed the swim—so there was plenty of time.

The three men watched a soldier, high up in the tower, toss the hooked rope towards the fence. After three attempts, the hook caught in one of the uprights and the soldier made the rope fast.

'Then I'll go,' Malik said. He shook hands with the Major, then turning to Smernoff, he said, 'This is the end of Girland. I warned him the next time we met, I would kill him.'

'Do you have to be so ambitious?' Smernoff asked, lowering his voice so the Major couldn't hear what he was saying. 'It is my job to kill Girland . . . I should go.'

'No . . . this is a personal thing between Girland and myself,' Malik said. He tossed away his cigarette butt, then offered his hand. 'Get those mines cleared.'

Smernoff shook hands.

'Good luck.'

He watched Malik stride to the watch tower and begin to climb the ladder to the upper platform. A few minutes later, he was high above Smernoff. He waved, then without hesitation, he took hold of the rope and began the long, dangerous slide down, controlling his speed with his legs. The rope sagged under his massive weight and Smernoff watched with alarm, but Malik reached the fence. He swung himself over the wire and dropped down on to Austrian soil.

He waved, then moving fast, keeping close to the fence, he started off for his rendezvous with Girland.

* * *

Captain Hugo von Raitenau, the Commander of the Austrian frontier post, reached for the telephone and asked to be connected to the American Embassy at Vienna.

As he waited for the connection, he leaned back in his chair, tapping his blotter with a pencil. Von Raitenau was some thirty-eight years of age, blond, tall and aristocratic. He had a rabid hatred of Communism, an admiration for the American way of life and a determination that was almost fanatical to snatch any fugitive who crossed the frontier out of the Communists' hands.

A voice told him he was through to the American Embassy.

The previous day, he had been alerted by Frank Howard, the C.I.A. agent working in Vienna that an American agent might be attempting to cross the frontier. Any news would be welcomed. Howard, a good friend of his, hadn't given him any details, but there was a hint that the crossing was important.

Howard came on the line.

'There has been an attempted crossing,' von Raitenau told him. 'I'm afraid it can't have been successful. The sound of exploding mines and machine gun fire have been reported. I am leaving immediately for the frontier. I will report back as soon as I get further information. Don't expect to hear anything for at least two hours.'

'I'll stand by,' Howard said. 'Thanks, Hugo. This is a top level affair. Can you give me a map reference where the crossing was attempted?'

'Section 15 . . . square 2,' von Raitenau told him.

'Okay . . . I'll stand by.'

* * *

During the past thirty-six hours, there had been considerable activity back in the American Embassy, Paris.

The news of Bruckman's death had finally reached Dorey. His contact in Prague at the American Embassy had sent a coded telegram. The news was brief and unsatisfactory. Bruckman had been shot. Girland, Worthington and Mala Reid were thought to be heading for the Austrian frontier. It was certain Malik and Smernoff were after them.

Dorey, pale, dark rings around his eyes, tossed the decoded telegram over to O'Halloran.

O'Halloran read the telegram and then dropped it on the desk.

'We don't know if Girland still has the document, do we?' he said. He pulled at his lower lip. 'I'm not worried about him. I'll back him any day against Malik and Smernoff.'

Dorey removed his glasses and began to polish them. This was always a sign that he was uneasy.

'It's three days now . . . do you think I should report that I've lost the document, Tim?'

'No. If it's lost, it's lost, but it is possible Girland will bring it out. Don't cut your throat too soon.'

Dorey brooded, then nodded.

'Yes. Well, at least, Latimer has gone in.' Seeing O'Halloran's look of surprise, Dorey went on, 'That was the operation, Tim. With Malik so tied up with Girland, I sent Latimer off yesterday morning. I've heard he had no trouble . . . so I haven't entirely messed up the affair.'

O'Halloran grunted.

'Girland could sell me down the river,' Dorey said bitterly. 'If he has the document and if he gets cornered by Malik he will bargain for his life with the document. He has no scruples . . . no principles.'

'Why shouldn't he make a bargain?' O'Halloran asked quietly. 'Have we ever done anything to encourage his loyalty?'

Dorey stiffened and stared at O'Halloran, then as he found nothing to say, O'Halloran went on, 'I'm going right away to Vienna. I've already alerted Howard who says there is a good guy in charge of the frontier post and he'll give us all the help he can.'

'All right, Tim,' Dorey said. 'I've got to get that T.S. back. I don't have to tell you . . . I'm relying on you.'

'If it can be got back, it will be got back,' O'Halloran said, and left the room.

In under the hour, he was in a fast military jet heading for Vienna.

* * *

Girland straightened up and wiped the sweat off his face with his forearm. He regarded the three oil drums now lashed together by rope. He wasn't happy about the rope. It was old and brittle, and he wondered if it would hold once the drums were in the water. He didn't let Mala know of his doubts. He grinned at her as he said, 'How's that for a do-it-yourself job?'

'Will they float?' Mala asked, staring uneasily at the drums and then looking at the oily, black water.

'Of course they will.' He squatted down on his heels and opened the rucksack. He emptied its contents. He found a plastic bag containing a lump of cheese, stale bread and a sausage. 'You must be hungry.'

Mala shuddered.

'I couldn't touch a thing.'

'Yeah . . . well, later perhaps.'

The smell of the water made him also feel queasy. He returned the food to the rucksack.

169

From his hip pocket, he took the soiled envelope with its Top Secret seal and put it in the plastic bag. From the rucksack he took the big packet of dollar bills. This was his and the Brauns' share of the thirty thousand dollars. He stuffed the money into the plastic bag. 'You'd better give me your money,' he went on. 'It'll be safer in this bag just in case we sink.'

Mala was now feeling cold. The dank atmosphere from the water was making her shiver. She put on her jeans and sweater, then taking the roll of money from her pocket, she handed it to him.

He made a secure parcel of the plastic bag, then put it back in the rucksack. He tied the straps of the rucksack to one of the ropes around the oil drums.

'Okay,' he said. 'Let's launch our boat.' He went to her and put his arms around her. 'Remember this: we are going to get out of here. That's understood. If something goes wrong, don't panic. Leave everything to me. We are going to eat the best and most expensive dinner in Paris three days from now.'

She held him close to her.

'I won't panic . . . promise.'

'Let's go.'

They kissed, then together they pushed the raft down the slope into the water. It floated easily. Girland picked up the automatic rifle and slid down the bank, catching hold of the raft and steadying it. Mala joined him.

'Get aboard,' Girland said, 'lie flat and keep to the off side.'

The drum dipped as Mala edged her way flat across the top of the drums. Girland held the raft steady and then crawled on and lay beside her. He had stuck the two candles on the foremost drum. The raft sank lower under his weight until it was just above the surface of the water.

'Well, at least it floats,' Girland said, then using the butt of the automatic rifle as a paddle, he moved the raft down the tunnel of water.

The rifle was heavy and Girland wondered how long he would be able to use it as a paddle. Four kilometres of water, Jan had told him. Well, they were on their way and

170

the raft was floating. But very soon, he felt a nagging ache developing in his back and he realised that he was wasting his strength using the rifle as a paddle.

'This isn't going to work,' he said and pulled the rifle out of the water. 'We'll use our hands.'

Suppressing a shudder, Mala dipped her hand into the filthy water. They began to paddle. The raft moved sluggishly, but it made progress. For more than half an hour, they continued to paddle with their hands and the raft continued to drift down the tunnel. Mala's arm was aching now, but she kept on. Looking up, Girland realised the dripping roof of the tunnel was closer and he guessed there was now more water in the tunnel than from where they had come. The air was getting bad. He could hear Mala gasping.

'Take a rest,' he said.

As she thankfully lifted her hand out of the water, she saw two glittering sparks close to her in the water. She jerked her hand up so violently, the raft wobbled.

'Steady,' Girland said. 'What is it?'

'There's something in the water!' She peered fearfully into the oily blackness but could see nothing.

Then Girland saw the twin sparks and snatched his hand out of the water as a big water rat made a pounce. It hit the side of the drums and recoiled.

Mala stifled a scream as she now saw the water was alive with rats.

Girland reached out and put his arm across her shoulders.

'Don't panic, honey,' he said. 'We'll get through,' but he was aware that the raft had come to a standstill. He could see in the flickering light of the candles that the water around them was swarming with vicious looking rats. He grabbed up the rifle and began to paddle with desperate strokes. The raft wobbled and then moved forward, its speed increased under Girland's frantic efforts.

A big rat, sleek with water, its eyes glowing, leapt out of the water and landed on the barrel of the gun. It snapped at Girland's hand, but he was just too quick for it. He struck it with his left hand, throwing it back into the water, then reversing the rifle, and aiming at the carpet of moving rodents, he pulled the trigger.

The noise of the exploding cartridge in the enclosed space was like a bomb going off. One moment there was a sea of rats around them: the next the rats had vanished. He could feel the great swirl of water as they dived and swam in panic away from the raft.

'Paddle!' he cried.

They began paddling with their hands but this time with a fast, exhausting stroke that sent the raft surging forward. But this pace couldn't last for long. Mala felt her strength draining out of her. In spite of forcing herself, her arm slowly lost power and finally she collapsed.

'I can't go on! I can't!' she sobbed weakly.

'All right, baby,' Girland said soothingly. 'Take a rest. Get your hand out of the water.'

They lay for some time, struggling to breathe. The raft drifted slowly forward. Then Girland felt something touch his shoulders. He stiffened, controlling the impulse to swing over on his back, knowing such a move might capsize the raft. Again something touched his back. Cautiously, he lifted his head and then realised that it was the roof of the tunnel scraping his shoulders as the raft drifted forward.

Was the tunnel ahead completely blocked by water? he wondered. Carefully, he turned on his back. He reached up and began to propel the raft forward by pushing against the slimy surface of the roof.

'Turn over,' he said. 'Be careful! The roof's right on top of us.'

Mala turned slowly. When she saw how close the roof was, she caught her breath sharply.

'We won't get through!' The edge of panic in her voice made Girland put his hand over hers.

'Come on, baby,' he said. 'You can help with this. We're getting out . . . it's a promise.'

He again began to push against the roof and Mala, stifling her panic, imitated him. The raft began to move forward at a much faster speed.

172

The air was very bad now. Every now and then, a projecting rock in the roof threatened to force the raft under water, but Girland managed to manoeuvre around it. Neither of them had any idea how long they continued to claw their way along the tunnel. Time stood still for them.

Scarcely able to breathe, sweat pouring from her body, Mala kept on. She had complete faith in Girland. He had said they would get out, and that meant they would get out.

But after what seemed to her to be an eternity, she felt her arms growing heavy. Her heart was racing. She made a desperate effort as she felt consciousness slipping away from her. Finally, her hands dropped and she collapsed into a huddled heap of despair.

Exerting his remaining strength, Girland kept pushing against the roof, sending the raft on and on into the evil smelling darkness. He too could scarcely breathe, and his efforts were becoming weaker. Then he found he had to reach further up to touch the roof. That could only mean the level of the water was dropping. He kept on. A few minutes later, his arms were fully extended and he was breathing more freely. Suddenly the roof was out of his reach and the raft began to lose momentum. He dragged himself on to his knees and again reached the roof. The raft tilted and he hurriedly adjusted its balance. He kept on until he had to stand to reach the roof, and then the roof was right out of his reach and a sudden breath of fresh air swirled around him. He lowered himself to lie flat on the raft and began paddling with his hands.

Mala stirred as the fresh air revived her.

'We're through,' Girland gasped. 'We've done it! Come on, sweetheart . . . start paddling!'

* * *

O'Halloran climbed from the military jet after it had landed at the Wein-Schwechat airport.

Frank Howard, the C.I.A. agent, ran across the tarmac and greeted him.

'I have a helicopter waiting,' he said. He was a tall, thin, youngish man with thinning hair and an aggressive jaw. 'Von Raitenau is expecting you. I'll brief you as we go.'

O'Halloran nodded and the two men walked across the tarmac to where a military helicopter was waiting. Once settled in their seats behind the pilot and as the machine became airborne, Howard said, 'Girland is trapped in a defunct copper mine. There are only two exits.' He went on to tell O'Halloran about Jan and Blanca Braun. 'I imagine Girland will try for the second exit. He'll be damn lucky if he breaks out. From what von Raitenau tells me the tunnel is full of water and man-eating rats, but he might just do it. Malik and Smernoff are handling the operation. This could be dodgy.'

O'Halloran was completely relaxed.

'I've known Girland for some time,' he said. 'He has this trick for survival. I'll bet you a hundred bucks he'll get through.'

Howard grinned and shook his head.

'No bet! I've heard plenty about Girland myself.'

The two men watched the ground slide under them as the helicopter pounded on towards the frontier.

* * *

Malik was getting worried. He had taken much longer than an hour to get within distance of the mine and now there seemed to be considerable activity on this side of the frontier.

Three times he had had to hide in the long grass as Austrian soldiers patrolled through the forest. Time was running out. It was now some minutes after four o'clock, and the sky was lightening.

For the moment the forest had become silent. Satisfied that the Austrian patrol had passed him, Malik stood up and began to move more quickly. In the distance he could see the outline of a derrick against the sky, and he knew he was at last approaching the entrance to the mine. But at this point, the forest petered out. He was now confronted by a large open space of rough grass and sand, and beyond, shrubs. He paused by a tree to listen. Somewhere to his right, he could hear men moving through the forest and a distant voice calling. He could see the mine shaft: a narrow tunnel overgrown by grass and shrubs. It would be from here that Girland would come if he came at all. Malik judged the distance and decided the range was too far for a certain shot with an automatic pistol. He would have to get closer: this would mean leaving his cover. Again he listened. The sound of movement and voices had died away. He hesitated, then ran fast across the grass and sand and plunged down behind a shrub. He waited for an alarm, but nothing happened. He surveyed the ground. To his left, growing on a small hillock was a thick clump of wild shrubs. From there, if Girland came from the tunnel, he would have a perfect shot at him. He ran to the hillock and flattened down on the sand behind the shrub. He took the heavy automatic pistol from its holster, slid back the safety catch and checked the magazine, then satisfied, he laid it on the sand within instant reach.

How long would he have to wait? he wondered. Maybe Smernoff had been right when he said he was crazy. The chances were Girland wouldn't succeed in escaping from the mine, then when the minefield had been cleared, the soldiers would move in to trap him. Again Malik heard distant voices. He looked towards the forest, but could see no movement. Then it dawned on him that if the Austrian troops remained in the forest, he could not risk shooting Girland. Even if he killed him, he himself would be trapped. The sound of the shot would bring the soldiers around him like a swarm of wasps and he would have no chance of getting back to the other side of the frontier.

Well, he would wait. He had no doubt, with his immense strength, he could kill Girland with his bare hands, but was he in the best position, should Girland come from the mouth of the tunnel? He surveyed the ground and decided he wasn't. He must make his way to the high ground above the mouth of the tunnel. From there he could drop on Girland as he came out.

As the sun came up behind the trees, Malik cautiously began to edge towards the new position.

The raft bumped gently against the bank. Ahead of him, Girland could see daylight. Fresh air, pouring down the mine shaft, cooled his exhausted, sweating body.

'We've arrived, baby,' he said. 'We're in Austria.'

Mala lay flat on her back, too tired, too exhausted to care. She was streaked with dust, her jeans were plastered to her body, her hair in long wet rat-tails.

'Come on, sweetheart,' Girland said. 'We've arrived.'

He slid off the raft into the filthy water and hauled the raft up on to the sandy bank. His body ached and he felt frighteningly weak, but he didn't care: they had won through.

Mala made the effort and reaching for his hand, dragged herself off the raft. They lay side by side, breathing the cool air and resting. They remained like that for some minutes, then Girland stirred himself. Getting up, he untied the rucksack from the raft. Their difficulties weren't over yet, he told himself. He had no idea what their reception would be when they encountered the frontier guards. He had no idea how far away they were from the nearest village or town.

'Feel like moving?' he asked, bending over Mala who lay flat on her back, her eyes half open.

She regarded him and smiled.

'You're a wonderful man. I'm so grateful to you.'

'The civic reception can come later,' Girland said. 'Come on . . . up on your feet.'

She gave him her hand and he pulled her to her feet.

'I must look a sight,' she said ruefully.

He laughed.

'I've seen worse, but not much worse.' He picked up the rifle and the rucksack. 'Let's go.'

Slowly, side by side, they walked up the long tunnel. Ahead of them, they could see a small circle of blue sky. When they finally reached the mouth of the tunnel, Girland stopped, putting his hand on Mala's arm.

'Stay here. I'm taking a look around. We don't want to get shot by some trigger-happy Austrian.' He laid down the rifle and the rucksack. 'When I'm satisfied it's safe, I'll be right back.'

'No! Don't leave me!' Mala's eyes widened with fear. 'Let me come with you.'

'Do what I tell you,' Girland said. 'I must see first if it is safe.'

The tone of his voice quelled her rising panic.

'All right . . . I'll wait.'

He regarded her affectionately. Although she was dirty, bedraggled and woebegone, there was this thing about her that made her special to him. He gave her a little hug.

'I'll be right back.'

He moved cautiously to the opening of the mouth of the tunnel. He stood for some time looking across the rough grass, the shrubs and the sand. There was a brooding silence over the distant forest. The sun made shadows. Lazy white clouds floated in the blue sky. It looked very peaceful out there, but Girland had learned never to take anything on its face value.

He remained still, listening. No sound came to him. Well, it looked safe, he told himself, and was about to call to Mala when he stiffened to attention. A few metres from him, he saw a footprint in the sand. He studied it, then looked for other prints, but couldn't see any more. Someone had been here, had moved from one grass tuft to another and had probably slipped and made this print before recovering and getting back to the grass.

Girland moved back. One footprint! This could only mean the man who had come here had been anxious to leave no trace of his approach. He again studied the print: the impression was deep and big: therefore a big, heavily built man. Girland became very alert. A big, heavily built man . . . Malik? Again he studied the ground. He could see nothing suspicious.

Could it be Malik? Had he crossed the frontier, knowing there was this exit from the mine? Girland nodded. Yes, Malik would take such a risk.

He returned to where Mala was waiting.

'I think we have trouble,' he said in a low voice. 'I don't

177

know for sure, but I think Malik is out there waiting for us.'

Mala caught hold of his hand.

'Take it easy,' Girland said. 'We can handle this.' He picked up the automatic rifle. 'Have you ever used one of these?'

She stared at him, her eyes dark with fear.

'No.'

'It's simple enough./Here, take hold of it.' He pushed the gun into her shaking hands. 'All you have to do is to point it and keep your finger hard on the trigger. It will fire twenty continuous rounds. Understand?'

She nodded dumbly.

'Here's what to do. I'm going out there. You come to the mouth of the tunnel. Point the gun at the sky and as soon as I'm in the open, press and hold back the trigger. Watch out. The gun will be hard to hold. The idea is to distract Malik's attention until I can spot where he is. The noise will also alert the frontier guards.'

While this was going on, Malik had seen Girland's shadow as he had come nearly into the open. He could hear him talking. He decided to make the first move.

Girland was saying, 'Got it all? Okay, don't be scared. All you have to do . . .'

'Don't move!' Malik barked. He appeared at the mouth of the tunnel, his pistol covering both Girland and Mala.

Mala dropped the rifle and screamed.

Girland grinned wryly.

'I had an idea you were around,' he said. 'You're sticking your thick neck out crossing the frontier, aren't you?'

'Come out here,' Malik said and began to move back into the open, still covering them. 'The girl stays where she is. You come, Girland. I want you.'

Girland's mind worked swiftly. Malik could have shot them both without them even knowing he was there. Why hadn't he? Obviously, being on the wrong side of the frontier, he would know at the sound of a shot, he would be trapped. So, the gun in Malik's hand was bluff. He dare not shoot.

Girland regarded him.

'Run away,' he said. 'If you're lucky, you might just get back to the other side. Go on, Comrade, get lost!'

Malik studied him. He realised that Girland knew the gun was a bluff.

'I warned you the next time we met, it would be the last time,' he said. 'Come out here.'

Although Girland was ready for Malik, he wasn't prepared for the speed this giant could move. With a quick flick, Malik tossed the gun from him and came at Girland with a charging rush. It was like the spring of a wild cat. He had the advantage of being on higher ground. Girland was badly placed. Malik hit him with his body, sending him crashing flat on his back. As Malik made a grab at Girland's throat, one of his long legs swept Mala off her feet, sending her flying backward to land with a splash and a scream into the oily water.

The grip on Girland's throat was like a vice. Savage, thick fingers dug into his windpipe. Malik was some ten kilos the heavier and Girland was completely flattened. While the breath in his lungs lasted, and he knew it could only last a few seconds, he slashed at the side of Malik's neck with a chopping Karate blow. Malik relaxed his grip and reared back, then smashed his clenched fist down towards Girland's face, but Girland, breath streaming back into his lungs, shifted his head in time and Malik's fist slammed down on the stone ground. He caught his breath in a gasp of agony as the bones in his hand shattered. Girland chopped him again and Malik fell away from him. Girland tried to struggle up, but his strength had gone. He managed to roll away from Malik and the two men lay on their sides, staring at each other. Slowly, his left arm hanging by his side, Malik got to his feet. He looked down at Girland.

Girland lay still. It was as if he were bloodless. The journey through the tunnel and the struggle had drained all the strength out of him.

Malik moved closer. He lifted his heavy boot with the intention of smashing it down on Girland's upturned face, then he hesitated. Why make a mess on his boot? He turned to look for a stone and found himself facing Mala,

179

dripping wet, covered in oil, her eyes staring, the automatic rifle held firmly in her hands.

Seeing her wild, desperate expression, Girland cried,
'Don't kill him!'

'I'm going to!' she sobbed.

'Mala!'

The snap in Girland's voice stopped her. She backed
away as Girland dragged himself to his feet. He joined her
and took the rifle from her.

Malik watched them. He braced himself, expecting Girland would kill him. His shattered hand was beginning to
swell, but his stone-like face was cold and expressionless as
he stared fixedly at the rifle.

Girland regarded him, then shook his head.

'Relax, Comrade,' he said. 'I'm not shooting you. Like
me, you do a job and like me, you are a sucker to do it.
That's the way it is.' He pointed to the raft. 'That's your
best way home. Watch out for the rats. It's some journey,
but I did it . . . so can you. Get going.'

Malik regarded him, his green eyes puzzled.

'I was going to kill you,' he said. 'What's the idea?'

'You take your job too seriously,' Girland said. 'Just because you were going to kill me doesn't mean I have to kill
you, does it?'

Malik paused to consider this, then he again regarded
Girland who waved him to the raft.

'Go on . . . shove off,' Girland said.

Still Malik studied him, then he said, 'We'll meet again.
When we do, I'll buy you a drink.'

Girland knew this was Malik's way of thanking him and
he grinned.

'That's a date. Wait a moment.' He turned to Mala. 'Get
his pistol.'

She stared at him.

'What do you mean?'

'Get his pistol, baby.'

She hesitated, then ran up the tunnel, found the automatic pistol Malik had thrown away and returned.

Girland took it from her, then walked to the water's
edge.

'You won't get far without a gun. The rats don't like noise,' and he offered the gun, butt first to Malik.

Malik made no move. He looked intently at Girland.

'I've always thought you were mad,' he said finally, 'now I'm sure of it.'

Girland laughed.

'That makes two of us. No one but mad men would do the work we do.'

He again offered the gun.

'That gun's loaded,' Malik said.

'So what? It wouldn't be much use if it wasn't loaded, would it?'

'You are giving me a loaded gun?' There was a bewildered expression in Malik's eyes.

'Oh, come on!' Girland said impatiently. 'You won't get through without it. We're professionals . . . and we are both working in this shabby, dirty racket. There comes a time when we can forget the little stinkers at the top who pull the strings . . . take it.' He shoved the gun at Malik who took it.

Mala watched breathlessly. She wanted to scream. Now this awful blond giant would kill him. She looked frantically around for the automatic rifle.

Girland turned.

'Don't get worked up, baby,' he said and going to her, he put his arm around her shoulders. 'He and I just happen to be on the wrong side of the Curtain.' He looked back and waved to Malik who was motionless, the gun hanging by his side, watching them. 'So long, and good luck.'

Picking up the rucksack, leaving the rifle, his arm still around Mala, he led her to the opening of the tunnel and into the early morning sunshine.

* * *

Mavis Paul, Dorey's secretary, was clipping papers into a file when her office door pushed open and Girland wandered in.

At the sight of him, she blushed and looked quickly

181

around her desk for a suitable weapon. She had met Girland before and she knew he took liberties.

Girland looked very handsome. He was wearing a cream lightweight suit, a blood red tie and reverse calf ankle high boots.

'There you are,' Girland said and smiled at her, putting his big brown hands on the desk and gazing with rapt attention into her eyes. 'I've been counting the hours. Last night, I dreamed of you.'

Mavis's fingers closed around a long, heavy ruler.

'Mr. Dorey is waiting for you. Please go straight in.'

'It's sad that a beautiful girl like you should be so wrapped up with a silly, little man like Dorey,' Girland said sadly. At the same time he was watching the ruler. He had had one slap in the face from Mavis and knew she had surprising strength. 'You and I could have lots of fun together . . . how are you fixed? How about the day after tomorrow? A cosy dinner, and then I could show you my electric razor.'

'If you don't get in there fast, I'll hit you!' Mavis said fiercely, pushing back her chair.

Girland drew back.

'Some other time, perhaps? Well, all right. Sooner or later the inevitable must happen. You're wasting the best time of your life, baby.'

'Get in there!' Mavis said, brandishing the ruler.

'While I'm talking to the old goat,' Girland said, moving to Dorey's office door, 'take stock. Think about what you are missing. You and I could have an experience together that would put L.S.D. off the map.'

Her face scarlet, Mavis pulled the typewriter to her and began pounding the keys.

Girland wandered into Dorey's office, closing the door behind him.

Dorey sat at his desk. Looking at him, seeing his white, drawn face, the dark shadows under his eyes, Girland felt sorry for him, but he didn't show it.

'Hello, there,' he said, and walked to the visitor's chair and sat down. 'How are your ulcers?'

Dorey said, 'I could have had you arrested, Girland.

Right now, you could be in an Austrian prison. I have been lenient with you, but understand this . . . I'm not standing any nonsense from you.'

Girland looked at him, then laughed.

'Dorey . . . you really kill me,' he said. 'That bluff wouldn't scare a kid of five. You have your script muddled. You know, as I know, you didn't dare have me arrested because you know I would have talked and you would be, by now, out of a job. You like your job. There are times when I have to admit you do it quite well. Every now and then, your imagination runs away with you and you drop a clanger. You played me for a sucker and I fell for it. I took your bait and swallowed the hook. You didn't give a damn what would happen to me.' He paused and stared soberly at Dorey who looked away, then he opened the gold cigarette box on the desk and helped himself to one of Dorey's hand-made cigarettes. He lit it with the gold lighter. 'You wanted to square accounts with me because I made a sucker out of you on our last operation . . . fair enough. When I found you had boobed and had planted a genuine top secret document on me I was in two minds what to do. I finally decided I would bring it back to you. It would have been much easier to have torn it up and flushed it down the toilet. I suppose I am a bit of a sucker. You and I have worked together for some time. I have always regarded you as a conscientious dope. For some reason or other, you do a good job. I wouldn't like to see you lose it because I'm pretty sure your successor could be a bigger dope than you are and that would be a disaster.' He took from his wallet the dirty, oil-stained envelope with its top secret seal and dropped it on Dorey's blotter. 'There it is. I won't bore you with the details about how I got it out of Prague. It was a rough trip, but I made up my mind you should have it back . . . you now have it back.'

Dorey opened the envelope and examined the crumpled sheets of paper it contained. His face lightened, the sparkle that had been missing from his eyes for the past three days now returned. He slid the papers into a drawer and turned the key.

'Thank you,' he said. Sitting back, he stared woodenly at Girland. 'And now, what are your terms?'

Girland stubbed out his cigarette.

'What's the matter with you, Dorey? Are you getting that old? Do you imagine I would have given you those papers if I was going to make a bargain with you?'

'I am not a rich man,' Dorey said, placing his finger tips together and resting his elbows on the desk. 'I know what money means to you, Girland. Could we settle this for twenty thousand dollars?'

Girland looked at him and shook his head.

'So you're still afraid I'll talk?' he said. 'Listen, you silly old goat, don't you understand you are the salt in my stew? I can't imagine life in Paris without you cooking up some trick, make some stupid mistake and coming to me to help you out. Can't you get that fact into your small, suspicious mind? Paris without you would be like Paris without the Eiffel Tower.' He got to his feet. 'Anyway, I've had fun, found a girl and even Malik is going to buy me a drink when next we meet.' He walked to the door, paused and looked at Dorey who was staring at him, his face set, his eyes behind the lenses of his glasses bright. 'The next time you take me for a sucker, will be the last time . . . just remember that.'

Dorey said quietly, 'There will be no next time . . . and thank you.'

As Girland opened the door, Dorey said, 'Wait.'

Girland lifted his eyebrows.

'Now what?'

'What happened to that thirty thousand dollars?' Dorey asked, leaning forward. 'Have you got it?'

Girland burst out laughing.

'The same old Dorey . . . see what I mean? Like the Eiffel Tower . . . you never change,' and he left the office, closing the door.

Mavis was still typing. She didn't look up. Girland paused to study her. She was beautifully built and he liked her uptilted nose and the waves in her hair.

'Have you made up your mind, honey?' he asked, pausing by her desk. 'How about this date?'

Without looking at him, without pausing in her typing, she said curtly, 'That is the way out,' and she jerked her head towards the outer door.

'Tell me something confidentially,' Girland said, leaning close to her. Lowering his voice, he asked, 'Do you prefer girls to boys?'

As Mavis's hand slapped across his face, Girland gathered her in his arms. Her warm, yielding lips met his and her arms slid around his broad shoulders.

Dorey, coming out of his office, paused, stared, hesitated, then silently stepped back and closed the door.

* * *

A taxi stopped outside Le Grand Vefour, one of France's eleven greatest restaurants that hid itself under the shadows of the arches of the Palais Royal.

Raymond Oliver, owner of this restaurant, tall, bearded, came to welcome Girland as Girland pushed open the glass door and stood aside for Mala to precede him.

The Maître's eyes ran over Mala, radiant in a white, simple evening dress and he approved, then he clasped Girland's hand warmly.

'It is a great pleasure to see you again, mon ami,' he said. 'Everything has been arranged. You have Colette's table.'

He led the way through the red plush and mirrored room to a table. Mala followed the tall figure, awed and excited. Life in Paris, after her years behind the Iron Curtain, had gone to her head like champagne.

Settled on the red plush, surrounded by expensively dressed Americans, they listened as Oliver described the menu while Henocq, the veteran wine waiter, placed vodka martinis on the table.

'Monsieur has already ordered,' Oliver said to Mala. 'There is toast de crevettes Rothschild, partridge, a little cheese and Coupe Empire. There is a Chablis 1959 and a Petrus 1945 for the grouse. Champagne, of course, for the dessert.'

Mala looked at Girland and put her hand on his.

185

'It sounds like heaven.'

'It'll taste like heaven, too,' Girland said.

It was some minutes before they were alone. Mala was very conscious she was looking her best. She had spent all the afternoon preparing for the occasion and when she looked at Girland, she could see his admiration.

Girland had booked a room for her at the Normandy Hotel, near the Palais Royal. When she arrived at the hotel room, she found it full of flowers. She had wept a little because this was happiness she had never known. Girland had called for her in a taxi and now they were in this restaurant. He had promised her the best and the most expensive dinner in Paris and although she had had faith in him, she hadn't really believed the time would eventually come when she would be sitting by his side in the quiet and safety of red plush and gilded mirrors.

It was after they had finished the crevettes Rothschild that Girland told her about Worthington's will.

'You have only to go to Geneva and to Credit Suisse Bank and tell them who you are to take over his money . . . it's quite a sum . . . sixty thousand dollars. It's all yours.'

'He really left it to me?' Mala asked, her eyes opening wide.

'Yes.' Girland sipped the Chablis. He watched her, wondering what was going on in her mind.

'He loved me,' she said. 'He was odd . . . a man I couldn't love.' She fingered the porcelain ash tray made from a cast of Colette's hand. 'What am I going to do with all that money . . . alone?'

'Ask the bank to invest it for you,' Girland said. 'You won't be alone for long.'

She hesitated, then said quietly, 'You wouldn't come to Geneva with me . . . we could be happy together.'

Girland shook his head.

'No..I'm a loner, baby. I can only thrive on my own.'

The partridge came, golden brown on its bed of foie gras and toast. The Petrus was poured.

Girland had a sudden feeling the evening was dying on him. He sensed Mala was close to tears.

Women! he thought. I wish I hadn't started something here. I should have known she would fall in love with me. Anyway, she has money, she is young and when she gets to Geneva she will find a new life.

Later, they left the restaurant. It had been a splendid meal, impeccably served, but the mood just wasn't there. They settled silently in the taxi that took them to the hotel.

As the taxi pulled up, Mala asked, 'Are you coming up?' Her warm hand closed over his.

This is the moment to stop, Girland thought. I must be free. I must be fair to her.

'No,' he said. 'Tomorrow you fly to Geneva and you will become a rich woman.' He took from his wallet the Air France ticket and dropped it in her lap. 'Make your own life, baby. You'll manage. A lovely with your looks and money won't be lonely for long.'

He leaned across her and opened the taxi door. 'Forget about me. I'm no good for any girl.'

She took the air ticket and pushed it into her bag, then she got out of the taxi. She peered down at him as he looked up at her.

'Thank you for the beautiful dinner,' she said. 'When next we meet, I'll buy you a drink.'

Girland laughed.

'That's my girl. So long, and good luck.'

She stared at him for a long moment, then turning, she walked slowly to the entrance of the hotel. Girland watched her, seeing the way she swung her neat little hips, her slim, upright figure very desirable.

'Where to?' the taxi driver asked, turning to look impatiently at Girland.

Girland was still watching Mala as she moved through the revolving doors. He remembered the moment in the cave when they had come together. He remembered that exciting little cry as he had entered her.

He felt a violent surge of desire to have that experience again.

'Where to?' he said. 'Why, nowhere,' and he dropped a ten franc note into the driver's hand and getting out of the taxi he hurried into the hotel lobby.

187

Mala was getting her key as Girland joined her.

She turned and they looked at each other, then smiling happily, she linked her arm in his and led him towards the elevator.

THE END

DO ME A FAVOUR, DROP DEAD
by James Hadley Chase

Keith Devery arrived in the small town of Wicksteed with a criminal record and a lot of ambition. And when he met Frank Marshall, a local drunk who was about to inherit a million dollars, he knew that here was a golden opportunity to get back into the big league. Marshall's mysterious wife Beth agreed with him . . . and together they ruthlessly plotted the perfect murder. Then Keith found that he had himself been set up . . . and that Beth had plans of her own once the money was hers . . .

'The thriller maestro of the generation'
Manchester Evening News

0 552 10574 0   £1.50

NO ORCHIDS FOR MISS BLANDISH
by James Hadley Chase

When Dave Fenner was hired to solve the Blandish kidnapping, he knew the odds on finding the girl alive were against him – the cops were still looking for her three months after the ransom had been paid. And the kidnappers, Riley and his gang, had disappeared into thin air. But what none of them knew was that Riley himself had been wiped out by a rival gang – and the heiress was now in the hands of Ma Grisson and her son Slim, a vicious killer who couldn't stay away from women . . . especially his beautiful new captive. By the time Fenner began to close in on them, some terrible things had happened to Miss Blandish . . .

One of the classic thrillers of all time.

0 552 10522 8   £1.50

THE JOKER IN THE PACK
by James Hadley Chase

When Herman dies, she thought, I will inherit sixty million dollars and I will be free to do just what I like. I can have any man I want . . . when he dies!

Sun-soaked Nassau . . . Helga Rolfe, flying in to join her elderly millionaire husband, Herman, found plenty of bad news awaiting her. Crippled, suspicious Herman, guessing how she's played around since their marriage, had decided to put a tail on her – and was proposing to write some nasty looking terms into his will . . .

Herman was right, of course – Helga's weakness was for handsome, sexy men – men like Harry Jackson, who she met on the beach the day she arrived. But Harry was not quite what she thought – and because of him she found herself in a nightmare world of blackmail, voodoo and violence.

0 552 10426 4   £1.50

COME EASY – GO EASY
by James Hadley Chase

When Chet Carson broke jail, he thought he'd found a safe hide-out in a lonely filling station. But instead he found himself caught up in a dangerous threesome – an elderly owner, his gorgeous wife Lola, and a safe with a fortune inside, which Lola wanted. Her chance came when she stumbled on Chet's identity and threatened him: 'Open the safe, or go back to jail.'

Chet was in dead trouble. They'd crucify him if he landed in prison again. But if he opened the safe, she'd pin the rap on him anyway. Somehow there had to be a third way . . .

0 552 11646 7   95p

MALLORY
by James Hadley Chase

A small French resistance group came to London after the war to avenge the death of their leader, betrayed to the Gestapo by one of their own members. But the traitor, Mallory, proved more than a match for them, and two corpses later, the remaining three called in outside help. They chose Martin Corridon, an ex-commando, who accepted the job planned a neat double-cross of his own once he had the money. But it didn't quite work out that way: Corridon found himself trailing Mallory from the dens of Soho to the wilds of a remote Scottish island . . .

0 552 10765 4   £1.75

AN ACE UP MY SLEEVE
by James Hadley Chase

An Ace Up My Sleeve is a story of a blackmail. It is a story of three people, all out for one thing: all determined to do anything to get it.

It is a story of bluff and counter-bluff – a game which develops into a deadly battle of violence and extortion.

From the moment Helga Rolfe, the elegant wife of one of the richest of tycoons, picks up a gum-chewing boy, young enough to be her son, events jump, bank and skid through a series of 180 degree turns and hair-raising gambits, racing to a climax of shattering impact – for both winners and losers . . .

0 552 09424 2   £1.75

CRIME TITLES AVAILABLE
FROM CORGI BOOKS

WHILE EVERY EFFORT IS MADE TO KEEP PRICES LOW, IT IS SOME-
TIMES NECESSARY TO INCREASE PRICES AT SHORT NOTICE. CORGI
BOOKS RESERVE THE RIGHT TO SHOW NEW RETAIL PRICES ON
COVERS WHICH MAY DIFFER FROM THOSE PREVIOUSLY ADVERTISED
IN THE TEXT OR ELSEWHERE.

THE PRICES SHOWN BELOW WERE CORRECT AT THE TIME OF GOING
TO PRESS (February '86).

☐ 10426 4	**JOKER IN THE PACK**	*James Hadley Chase*	£1.50
☐ 11558 4	**WELL NOW MY PRETTY**	*James Hadley Chase*	£1.50
☐ 11356 5	**THE WAY THE COOKIE CRUMBLES**	*James Hadley Chase*	£1.50
☐ 10522 8	**NO ORCHIDS FOR MISS BLANDISH**	*James Hadley Chase*	£1.50
☐ 10574 0	**DO ME A FAVOUR, DROP DEAD**	*James Hadley Chase*	£1.50
☐ 11646 7	**COME EASY, GO EASY**	*James Hadley Chase*	95p
☐ 11506 1	**BELIEVED VIOLENT**	*James Hadley Chase*	£1.50
☐ 11042 6	**CONSIDER YOURSELF DEAD**	*James Hadley Chase*	£1.95
☐ 09648 2	**HAVE A CHANGE OF SCENE**	*James Hadley Chase*	£1.75
☐ 10765 4	**MALLORY**	*James Hadley Chase*	£1.75
☐ 09424 2	**AN ACE UP MY SLEEVE**	*James Hadley Chase*	£1.75
☐ 10328 4	**LADY, HERE'S YOUR WREATH**	*James Hadley Chase*	£1.75

*All these books are available at your book shop or newsagent, or can be ordered
direct from the publisher. Just tick the titles you want and fill in the form below.*

CORGI BOOKS, Cash Sales Department, P.O. Box 11, Falmouth, Cornwall.

Please send cheque or postal order, no currency.

Please allow cost of book(s) plus the following for postage and packing: **U.K.**

Customers—Allow 55p for the first book, 22p for the second book and 14p for each
additional book ordered, to a maximum charge of £1.75.

B.F.P.O. and Eire—Allow 55p for the first book, 22p for the second book plus 14p
per copy for the next seven books, thereafter 8p per book.

Overseas Customers—Allow £1.00 for the first book and 25p per copy for each
additional book.

NAME (Block Letters) ....

ADDRESS ....

....